Archangel

Ed Adams

a firstelement production

First published in Great Britain in 2020 by firstelement
Copyright © 2020 Ed Adams
Directed by thesixtwenty

10 9 8 7 6 5 4 3 2 1

A CIP catalogue record for this book is available from the
British Library.

ISBN 13 : 978-1-8380146-4-3

Ebook ISBN : 978-1-8380146-5-0 (Amazon)

Printed and bound in Great Britain by Ingram Spark

rashbre
an imprint of firstelement.co.uk
rashbre@mac.com

Mailing list: https://mailchi.mp/9f0b30712620/ed_adams

"þetta reddast"

things always have a way of working out in the end

Icelandic credo

THANKS

A big thank you for the tolerance and bemused support from all of those around me. To those who know when it is time to say, "step away from the keyboard!" and to those who don't.

To thesixtwenty.co.uk for direction.

To anyone who has read any of the Triangle trilogy

And, of course, thanks to the extensive support via the random scribbles of rashbre via http://rashbre2.blogspot.com and its cast of amazing and varied readers whether human, twittery, smoky, cool kats, photographic, dramatic, musical, anagrammed, globalized or simply maxed-out.

Not forgetting the cast of characters involved in producing this; they all have virtual lives of their own.

And of course, to you, dear reader, for at least 'giving it a go'.

Books by Ed Adams include:

- **The Triangle:** Dirty money? Here's how to clean it
- **The Square:** Weapons of Mass Destruction – don't let them get on your nerves
- **The Circle:** The desert is no place to get lost
- **The Ox Stunner:** *The Triangle Trilogy* – thick enough to stun an ox
- **Coin:** Get rich quick with Cybercash – just don't tell GCHQ
- **Pulse:** Want more? Just stay away from the edge
- **Edge:** Power can't be left to trust
- **Archangel :** Sometimes I am necessary

TABLE OF CONTENTS

PART ONE

Author's Note

This book is an attempt to piece together the story of Christina Nott, variously known by a multiplicity of other names in her past.

We sat together while this was being created and much of what is written is exactly as it was spoken into the Philips Voice Tracer and then transcribed into Dragon Dictate.

I've cleaned up the wording somewhat and occasionally skipped a graphic moment, but most of what is in the following pages is as Christina intends it to be. I guess you'd call it an autobiography, although Christina sometimes thinks of it as notes on part of a life.

She's changed identity again now, so there's no direct way to pin her to this and I've been asked by lawyers to describe the whole thing as a work of fiction, which gets around several matters, which will be resolved as the story unfolds.

Starting Out

"WHAT YOU WON'T FIND IN HER CLOSET

- *Three-inch heels. Why live life halfway?*
- *Logos. You are not a billboard.*
- *Nylon, polyester, viscose and vinyl will make you sweaty, smelly and shiny.*
- *Sweatpants. No man should ever see you in those. Except your gym teacher – and even then.*
- *Leggings are tolerated.*
- *Blingy jeans with embroidery and holes in them. They belong to Bollywood.*
- *UGG boots. Enough said."*

— Anne Berest, How To Be Parisian

Agnes Örnólfsdóttir

We are in Iceland at the start. Agnes was born to the Örnólfs and gained the name Agnes Örnólfsdóttir. On Iceland, the last names of everyone reflect their family and so Örnólfsdóttir literally means Örnólf's daughter.

It shouldn't be mistaken for Guðmundsdóttir, which is famously the last name of Björk Guðmundsdóttir and is probably the only Icelandic person who many can name.

Christina continues: I guess there's a couple of footballers too, Gylfi and Kolbeinn. Then I could list Vigdís Finnbogadóttir as president of Iceland in 1980. She was the first female in the world to win a national presidential election. She was re-elected a further 3 times.

Or Hafþór Júlíus Björnsson, best known as 'The Mountain' in the Game of Thrones series. And still, in popular culture, we can't forget the PlayStation. Ólafur Jóhann Ólafsson was responsible for its introduction.

But we're better off to think of Iceland as the land of the ice and snow.

As Jimmy Page and Robert Plant described it:

We come from the land of the ice and snow. From the midnight sun, where the hot springs flow. The hammer of the gods. We'll drive our ships to new lands, to fight the horde, and sing and cry, 'Valhalla, I am coming!'

Yes, Immigrant Song, famously written after the Zep toured into Reykjavik. Shop assistants in Reykjavik wear the lyrics on tee-shirts to this day.

I was not an immigrant in Iceland. It is where I'm from, but I've moved so many times I feel like an immigrant everywhere now. At least I do not feel *of* the place. More like an outside observer.

I can only remember a few events from my time in Iceland. We lived on a smallholding with a selection of sheep and horses. If it sounds in any way glamorous, it was not. My Pabbi worked the land and managed the animals. The horses were the typical Icelandic type, which sometimes people mistake for ponies. They taught me to ride from an early age and have memories of being on a horse, helping Pabbi bring in the sheep.

I am sure that's what has toughened me to the elements too, Iceland was cold, and very snowy. When the winds blew it could be icy, yet the overall climate was well-tempered. Mamma used to put me outside when I was a little elskan, in all weathers. I have since heard that this was considered cruel by some people, but the culture in Iceland is to do this and ensure the baby gets fresh air.

Our place was about three hours outside of Reykjavík on

the F35, sandwiched between two glaciers. There was always a view out towards ice both to the east and to the west, although Pabbi said that the eastern ice was melting quickly.

It meant that in my early years I learned from the land. How to read the skies, of animals and their ways and their tracks. We had a small local school, but I was told that I would need, at some point, to go to a big city for my education.

In the evening, indoors, we would sing songs, and I learned to play the piano, except I could not reach down to the pedals on the old upright piano that we had.

I discovered that my other source of learning was the television. The Americans had an Air Force base at Keflavik, and they'd installed a huge aerial that transmitted American television to the whole of Iceland. I think it was to make the Americans feel at home when they transferred to Iceland, but it also meant that most of Iceland learned English from the broadcasts. We also learned about a lot of American products which we could not get in Iceland, but that the Americans had flown in on their transport planes.

I could play many of the jingles from the television on the piano. At one time, as children, we even formed a small band who practiced together in one of the bedrooms of the farm-house. I think it was a subtle way that Mamma ensure we had music lessons.

I had not accounted for Pabbi's other job. As well as his business as a smallholder, unknown to me he was paid to watch the sky. One of our farm sheds was off-limits to me. When I had friends around to play, we were told never to go into the Ullarverslun - the wool store. I was told I was allergic and that it would make me ill.

The threat of illness was enough to keep me away until one day when we were playing some kind of hide-and-seek game. Hekla - my best friend - had run towards the Ullarverslun and made as if she was going to hide somewhere near it. We were past the window weather and into the warm summer months with bright sunshine.

There was a sudden crack, and a piece of timber fell from the store. It turned out Hekla was trying to climb over the top of the door to a flat area of roof, where she could both hide and catch some sunlight.

Instead, she fell through the roof and into the building. It wasn't much of a drop, maybe two metres in total, and she knew to lower herself through the gap so she'd only need to drop about a metre. No problem for a nine-year-old.

Then she came back to the door and opened it. I was expecting to see wool piled up from floor to ceiling. I'd never really thought about it being any different.

Sure, we had sheep. Proper Icelandic sheep which did get woolly in the winter months. They were sheared by Pabbi and Kristján, who used to come up from the town to help. I'd never really thought about where the wool went, except that it was in the wool store.

So, it was a surprise to finally see inside the store. It looked electrical. There were several boxes with lights flashing, a desk and a computer terminal.

There was also what looked like a huge satellite dish, pointing upwards, although there was a roof above it.

Hekla was as surprised as I was.

"Is your dad a spy?" she asked.

"No," I said, "He's an astronomer - a man who looks at the stars."

Even at this young age, I was adept at ad-libbing and the American television we picked up had given me even more ideas.

"We'd better tell Pabbi," I said, "Don't worry, I know how to explain this - let me do the talking."

Hekla was very frightened in case Pabbi was angry. She asked if it would be all right if she left early that day. I knew that she was not allowed to walk across the fields alone and that she would have to wait for her Mamma to pick her up in the car.

We went back to the house, and I found Pabbi repainting a water trough. He could tell that something was wrong and asked what it was.

I told him we'd accidentally broken the roof of the Ullarverslun, and he looked concerned.

"Are you both okay?" he asked, "No bangs and scrapes?"

We both nodded, and Pappi looked less annoyed than we had expected.

"I was worried about that roof," he said, "It needs fixing - I hope now you'll remember to stay away from there."

He looked at both Hekla and me and could see that we were both breathing and didn't look more scratched than normal.

"Let me tell Mamma about this," he said.

And then he carried on with his painting.

Well, Hekla and I ran back outdoors, "I wasn't expecting that," said Hekla, "My dad would have been furious if I'd smashed one of his sheds. Even if it needed fixing."

I pretended that Pabbi was cool, but really I wondered if he'd been nice because of Hekla being around to play.

That night-time, it was time for bed and Pabbi's turn to tuck me in. He asked me a question, "Today, when Hekla fell through the shed, did either of you notice what was inside?" he asked.

"We did," I said to Pabbi, "It looked like a telescope or something,"

"Yes, they have asked me to look after it for some men who live a long way away." He replied.

"They asked me to keep it a secret, actually,"

"Why's that Pabbi?" I asked.

"Well, they give us some money for the farm," he replied, "They just ask me to look through the telescope every so often." Then he kissed me on the forehead and left the room.

I wondered what it all meant, but I didn't have long to find out. A few days later Hekla's mother came around and was chatting to Mamma. They were in the kitchen. Hekla's mother said, "Thank you," to Mamma for being so nice the day that Hekla had fallen through the roof. She explained that Hekla had been worried about being told off. Mamma was very curious by this. She looked like she was hiding it but pretended to know what had happened. I could tell she was fibbing.

Then, at tea-time, Mamma and Pabbi talked about it some more. Pabbi looked worried that Hekla's mum knew about the wool-store.

"I'll have to report it, and then it will only be a matter of days," said Pabbi.

A few days later, some men in a big red car arrived at the farm. They said they were from the insurance company and would talk to Pabbi alone.

After they had left, Pabbi said he had a family announcement.

"We've been told by the men who visited today that we are such excellent farmers that they want us to show some other people how to do it."

Mamma looked sad, but I thought we had just won a prize.

"Yes, he said, we are invited to a new land to show people how to farm sheep."

"Where Pabbi, where?" I asked, hoping it would be America and that then we could get some of the items advertised on television.

"We are going to Russia," he said, "To Arkhangelsk- It is very like Iceland."

"Then why are we going?" I asked, "if it is just like here?"

"You will learn a new language," Pabbi said, "And you won't be confused by the climate."

"Will I still be able to watch American television?" I remember asking.

"No, but you will have a good selection of Russian television instead."

"Will people understand when I speak Icelandic?" I asked.

"No, but they will understand English, or at least some of them will."

I can remember being shocked by this, but also excited at the chance to go to Keflavik airport to catch a big plane to Russia. We were going to fly to Moscow and then catch a train for the last part of the journey.

"How far is it, ástin mín " Mamma asked Pabbi.

"From Moscow, it's about 1,200 kilometres. It's on the White Sea."

Mamma started crying. I think she was sad to be leaving Iceland.

Ed Adams

Leaving Iceland

Things moved quickly. The men who had visited in the red car came back.

I had to get a passport and have pictures taken.

Hekla came around to say goodbye. She said she wondered if it is because we had looked in the wool store that it meant I was going away.

I said we were going to a new country to teach people how to look after sheep. This impressed Hekla, but she also asked if they had American television.

The time came, and I had to say goodbye to the dogs and the horses. I was especially sad to say goodbye to my favourite horse, the wonderful Einar. The dogs seemed to sense that there was something happening, and we threw them more treats than usual. Our dogs were working dogs and they lived outside in kennels. The idea that they would get treats was especially unusual to them, because they had probably only ever received them when they were puppies.

Then a taxi arrived, and we climbed aboard. It was a big mini-bus and had space in the back for our luggage. I realised that we were leaving a huge amount behind and that we would need to start anew when we reached Archangel.

The plane ride was a thrill for me, and I was preoccupied with the airport, the fancy shops, unusual food and even some American goodies on offer. When we took off, I could see Keflavik below, then Reykjavik, and then we flew right over the glaciers. I looked at the gap between them and tried to work out where our farm was, but I couldn't see it.

We were flying with Islandair, and the plane had to stop over in Amsterdam. We were allowed to disembark, and I could look around the airport. It was huge and had shops and even a casino. We ate some pizza upstairs in a cafe before we continued with our flight. I asked Pabba how far it was, and he said the whole flight was 17 hours.

While we were at the airport, I listened out for other people speaking Icelandic, but I didn't hear anyone, apart from in the lines for our plane. Some spoke Norwegian and even Swedish and I could understand them both. I could not understand someone speaking Danish at all. But what I also noticed was just how many people spoke English. It differed from the American English on the television, although I decided I could understand that the best of all the languages being spoken.

We had different seats for the second part of the flight, although Mamma and Pabbi still let me have the window seat. I could see the patchwork of Europe spreading out in front of the plane until we were above the clouds. We seemed to be above the clouds for a long time but then, as we came through them, I could make out the first of what I realised was Russia.

Then some announcements in a new language (which I subsequently realised was Russian). We were in the flight path to Sheremetyevo International Airport.

We landed, and I remember the first sights. When we approached Keflavik airport, there was something that looked futuristic about its architecture. To me, it looked big too. But Sheremetyevo AS Pushkin was huge. Plate glass, it looked as if a spacecraft had landed. Sweeping curves of glass. This Russia was even more impressive than the America as I'd seen it on television.

We were soon out of the plane, and in an airport that seemed vaster than Schipol in Amsterdam. And Schipol had its own train station built into the airport as well!

Pabbi said we had to go to a special delegations' lounge where we would be met by some men. We followed the signs and soon arrived at a golden waiting room. On the way to the area I had noticed that there were several other VIP lounges too and each of them was even more golden than the last. I decided I would only fly from this airport if I could sit in the golden areas first.

We found the area, and everyone sat around a low table. The men were drinking something which I think might have been vodka. Pabbi and Mamma were asked if they would like drinks too, and they offered me some Coca-Cola. At least I could still get American things in Russia.

It turned out that the men were giving us some tickets for the train and also a stay in a hotel in central Moscow.

We would spend a day in Moscow before travelling to Archangel. I asked how long the train ride would be.

It shocked me to hear that it was 21 hours. The men showed me a picture of the train. It looked like something from America. It was streamlined, and bullet shaped. It looked as if it could travel very fast.

"Not only that," said Pabbi, "These tickets are for first class. We can travel this next piece in comfort." I looked over to Mamma. She looked as if she had been crying.

The men said they would get tickets to Moscow for us on the subway, but they thought it would be better to give us the cash instead. We could then get a taxi from outside directly to the hotel. It would be better than carrying our suitcases around the streets of Moscow.

Pabbi asked how much the taxi should be. The men told him, and he smiled. The taxis in Moscow were good value after the costs of taxis in Iceland.

Then we went to the place where the bags are unloaded. Another man was waiting there with our bags. They had unloaded them and put them into a trolley for us.

I decided that Pabbi must be thought of as important in Moscow to get this kind of treatment, with the golden lounge and then with the luggage. It startled me when the Russian announcements in the baggage hall also included one in Icelandic. I realised it was for our plane.

Then to the very centre of Moscow. What a city! It was so messy after Reykjavik. The traffic was unbelievable. It was also very polluted with car, and lorry fumes rising while we sat in still traffic. Some of the trucks seemed to have huge exhaust pipes that pointed out sideways at just the height of the windows in our taxi. A few cars with blue lights seem to dash past us, but they couldn't all be police.

In English, the taxi driver explained that the cars belonged to 'the Mafia' who could buy blue light passes.

The taxi driver said he had a brother in Chicago and that he was originally from Pakistan, which is where he had learned his English. He sounded different from the Americans I'd heard on television.

The hotel we were going to was a Radisson, which is a Swedish firm. We were expecting it to be like a lot of Swedish things with maybe some pine wood on display. It was a bit of a family joke and I suppose was part of the friendly tension between Iceland, Norway and Sweden.

How wrong we all were! The hotel turned out to be one of Stalin's skyscrapers in the centre of Moscow. It was more like a palace and had a river view.

The entrance lobby was all marble columns and had a floor like a mirror of marble patterns. There were chandeliers hanging from the ceiling.

We checked in and were then accompanied to our floor where we had two rooms with an adjoining door. I had my room on the top floor of a palace in the centre of Moscow!

We were told that we had the room booked for overnight and because our train was late in the day, we had it booked until the next evening!

The lady at the check-in also told us (in English) about

the hotel's boats which ran along the river and would give us a chance to see the city without getting tired. I don't think she knew how far we walked in an average farm-day!

A man took our bags to the rooms, and then we were ready to look around. Mamma looked tired, but I wanted to see this city. Pabbi suggested that we should all have a rest and then go to the river and catch a boat.

We went to our rooms, but I noticed that Pabbi and Mamma had a visitor for around 15 minutes. I think they were checking on our progress.

I watched some television, which had about a hundred channels including American and British, which I could understand and Russian, which I couldn't understand and seemed to be boring.

Then we left for the boat trip, all along the river under a glass canopy. Moscow was well lit from the boats and I thought we were making faster progress than we did in the taxi. Wherever I could see traffic, there seemed to be a jam.

The next day, we started with a good breakfast, of anything you could think of, and then decided to walk to Red Square and The Kremlin and on to St Basil's church. The previous evening we'd worked out that it was a short straight line to get to all of those sights, although the boat had wound its way there because of all the bends in the river.

It still took us about an hour to complete the walk, but it was very interesting to see the modern Russia at work, plus the scores of tourists in the Red Square.

Too soon it was time to collect our bags from the hotel and make our way to the train station, with another taxi. We could have walked it quicker than the taxi, although we'd have had to carry the big suitcases with us.

Then we arrived at the train station. It was a different feeling here. A much messier form of Russia and very limited signs in anything we could understand. We asked about the train to Arkhangelsk and were pointed towards a particular platform. We were going first class, remember.

Then came the shock. The train on the platform was an old one. Not a bullet train like in the picture, but an old set of silver-coloured carriages and a separate diesel engine. What's more, the journey wasn't 21 hours. It was now shown as 23 hours and with around 40 stops.

"Guð minn" said Mamma. I wasn't used to hearing her swear. She looked towards Pabbi and asked, "Are you sure this is the right train?" He looked at the tickets, the numbers on them and said, "Yes, I'm sure."

We edged along the train to find our compartment, hoping that things would get better.

They didn't. This was the standard train first-class compartment, roughly equivalent to 2nd class on a mainline train elsewhere.

"At least it is clean," I can remember Mamma saying, as she looked at the chairs and table.

It was a plain-looking carriage and we would be in it for a whole day, travelling to Arkhangelsk.

First Class explanation

The train ride was when Pabbi told me what was really happening. All three of us were seated at the table in the compartment of the train. Pabbi explained that we were being relocated by the Russian FSB. Pabbi had once been a pilot in Russia but had been asked to move to Iceland by his bosses.

He had suffered from stress as a consequence of flying military jets along the boundaries of other countries. The instructions were always to fly as close and low to the ground as possible, to escape radar detection. This was extremely tough flying and even in the latest Sukhoi SU-35s he had found it difficult to keep to the contours. At any moment he could trip an alarm and be subjected to anti-aircraft fire as well as setting off a diplomatic incident.

One day, his buddy Nikolay in the same flight had done just that and triggered a jet scramble from a Finnish F-18 Hornet, which he should have been able to outmanoeuvre. The Finnish plane had fired a warning shot across the front of the Russian, but he'd panicked and ejected from the flight. He'd landed in Finland and been repatriated.

Nikolay's plane had crashed into a field and created much wreckage but no injuries or fatalities. Nikolay had been a mental wreck after that and was threatened with court-martial for losing an expensive plane.

Pabbi said he realised that he was also burned out at the same time as Nikolay and sought to get out of the flying. He said he had done over 100 stressful sorties by this time.

The authorities had offered him the farm as an incentive for him to move and Pabbi had been pleased to accept. He had always dreamt of life as a farmer and this life away from everything seemed like his best option.

Pabbi had been dating Mamma at this time, and she had an Icelandic background, so they would select Iceland as the new location.

This was ideal for Pabbi, who knew he could then propose to Mamma and would have some property to his name. The chance for Mamma to get back to Iceland was additional incentive. That's why they had chosen the last name Örnólfs; it was Mamma's last name before she had moved to Russia with a fisherman, from whom she was now divorced.

So, do you have a Russian Name?" I asked Pabbi.

Pabbi looked at Mamma and said, yes, "Its Arnol'd. Arnol'd Miasnikow"

"Okay, so you will have to tell me about the wool store," I asked

"It was part of the deal," said Pabbi. "I was an ex-fighter pilot, so I knew a lot about aviation."

"The authorities wanted me to set up a listening station in the middle of Iceland. It was part of the deal for me to transfer out of the Air Force."

"I was to listen to the UN radio chatter and to monitor the planes circuiting through the area. Keflavik was still a big American base when we started out."

"So Hekla was right? - You were a spy?" I asked Pabbi.

"That's a strong word for what I was doing, " said Pabbi, "It was more like a plane spotter."

"But one that did it in secret?" I asked, still a little surprised by this whole thing.

"There's still more," said Pabbi, "There would have been trouble for me in Iceland, if I'd been picked up by the police. Your little friend might have accidentally said some things to her mother and that could have caused ripples which would alert the authorities."

"So, the Russians agreed to move us all out?"

"Mamma knows all of this, but - yes - they did offer," answered Pabbi, "But I wanted to make sure that you and Mamma would be all right too."

"Mamma already speaks Russian, and has lived here, so that isn't such a problem. But for you, dear Aggi, I wanted the best education and no chances lost."

"Because of my record in the Air Force and my time spent abroad doing the listening work, I'm regarded as something of a Russian hero back in Moscow. That is why I am being treated so well. That is why we all are being treated well.

The authorities have agreed to rehouse us all in very nice accommodation in Arkhangelsk, to offer me a farm-based job if I wish, but most importantly, to put you into the Academy in Arkhangelsk. That's the highest education establishment available and normally requires passing a special entrance examination. They say that the Academy is also holistic. It looks at the whole person mind, body and soul. Mamma and I are very proud that you will be able to go to this Academy."

I was taken aback. In the course of a couple of days, I'd said goodbye to my best friend, to my favourite horse, to my home, and I was now travelling across North West Russia in a train to a new home and life in an Academy.

"I can see this is a lot to take in," said Mamma, "We have thought long and hard from way before this happened about what we would do if such a situation occurred."

"We couldn't talk about it to you, in case you mentioned it to someone, see what happened when your best friend found out by accident - and we don't - in any way - blame her for any of this."

"It can be like a new start for us, your parents, and for you the beginning of a great adventure," said Pabbi.

Preparation

Пан или пропа́л.

To become a master or to be gone.

Russian Proverb

(up or out)

Agnessa Dobrayadoch

That was when Pabbi showed me my new Passport. It was Russian.

I wanted to see my picture. "Agnessa Dobrayadoch", it said.

"Is that me? " I asked.

"Yes Aggi, my dear, it is," said Pabbi.

Mamma nodded," We've all got new names," she said.

"So, are we the Dobrayadochs?" I asked, somewhat confused.

"That's right," said Pabbi, "The goodmans - Dobraya is good. Doch is Man"

"Like Björk Guðmundsdóttir," I said, "I'll be Goodman's daughter."

Agnessa is the Russian for Agnes. So, you keep your first name, We can still call you 'Aggi'.

"What about you?" I asked, "We had had to take this new last name so we can't be mistaken for the Russian people that we were when we left," explained Mamma.

So that's how I got my second name, Agnessa Dobrayadoch. At least it sounded Russian.

We travelled across a huge expanse of Russia, but I realised from a map that it was still only a tiny part of the vast country.

We travelled through forests, cleared for the train line and an accompanying road. Every so often, maybe every 50-100 kilometres, there was another small town and a train station. We always stopped, and I realised why the journey would take so long.

Then the train line started to follow a river and I could look out of both sides of the carriage to see the way the river changed sides as we crossed small bridges. The road was following a similar route but didn't seem to carry much traffic.

Occasionally I'd see a walled city, or a brightly painted church, like a miniature version of the one at St Basil's back in Moscow. Compared with Iceland, the land was very flat, with views across many miles. The river we crossed also seemed very brown, not like the glacier clear waters around our farmstead.

Most of the buildings by the railway track side seemed

very 'used'. They were industrial looking, coated with dust and looked as if they had a hard life.

Occasionally I could see large advertisements alongside the road or on hoardings by the side of the rail tracks. They seemed to advertise everything either literally (like a picture of an oil can) or with women holding it (car tyres, pizzas, soap powder, more oil cans). The women didn't seem to have much idea about what they should be wearing either.

I decided to grade adverts on the train to pass the time. I had a little notebook.

A good one was for some kind of food, which seemed to come in a selection of baskets.

A brash one was for a gold Rolex, which was about the size of the moon.

A repeating one was of a woman reading a newspaper. She looked like she was from the 1950s and I could work out that the advert was for Pravda.

A readable one was for Coca-Cola, usually as we approached the next town.

I saw several for what I thought were cigarettes too, but I later learned that these were an anti-smoking campaign that copied cigarette branding. Two cowboys in Marlborough hats with the slogan "Bob, I've got emphysema" or two 1950s film stars with the slogan "Mind if I smoke? - Care if I die?".

The Apartment

When the taxi arrived at our new home, I was quite shocked because of the size of the apartment block. I'd been used to living on a farm with several buildings, and the livestock. Here in Russia I'd been told we would be in an apartment. Most apartments I'd seen were in American TV shows, and quite spacious.

I realised quickly that housing in Russia is quite different from Europe or the U.S.

The first thing I realised was that we would be living up in the air. The twentieth floor, actually, and I was told that the apartment was larger than a typical one in Moscow, because we were out in Arkhangelsk, where there was more space.

We met a woman downstairs, and she showed us to the apartment. We caught an elevator to our floor, but I think we were all wondering what would happen if it went out of service. The woman was fairly quiet but spoke quite good English.

She told us that normal apartments were about 30 square metres, but we were moving to a 45 square metre two-bedroom apartment with a balcony. By Russian standards, this was well above average.

She showed us along the corridor and explained about the extra door in the corridor which was locked at night. It wasn't like a normal door, more like a metal gate. She explained it was added security and ensured that only the right people would be in the corridors.

She showed us the camera on the wall, which was linked to the entry phone system. "Extra security," she said.

It was so different from on the farm where we'd leave most of the doors unlocked and could tell if we had visitors right from when they came in through the main gate.

Pabbi must have been well thought of. When we walked into the apartment, I was also very surprised. I had expected it to be somehow "homely", but it was very modern and sleek. It didn't look as if anyone had lived there before. There was a washing machine which still had the stickers on it from the shop. There was a very large window in the lounge area, which looked out towards the water, although it was a couple of blocks to the shoreline.

If this apartment was in Reykjavik, it would have been very expensive. The kind of place that bankers lived.

I looked at Mamma and for the first time in ages I saw her smile. Pabbi looked relieved, too. I don't know if it is just because we had arrived, or whether they were also worrying about where we would live.

Now, compared with our kitchen on the farm, the kitchen here was small, but it had all the essential items.

A hob, oven, microwave and even a dishwasher. They were all condensed into a small space, but somehow it didn't matter because they looked somehow 'cool'.

Then we looked at the two bedrooms. They were both almost the same size, although one had better windows, that went from floor to ceiling and let in lots of light. It looked as if the glass opened and there was access to the same balcony that went around to the lounge too.

I guessed that's where my parents would go. The other room was a similar size, but the smaller window looked out across the city and I could see the sea. It had a built-in storage cupboard. Big enough that I could stand up inside of it.

Then the bathroom had a large bath and a quite fancy looking shower. Along one wall ran a huge mirror and some lights that were hidden behind it and came on when we flipped a switch. It was like something from Hollywood.

The bathroom didn't have the toilet in it. Instead, there was another small room which had the toilet. It seemed unusual, but the woman said it was considered a privilege to have a separate toilet in the apartment.

We also didn't have the usual kind of lights. We had spotlights in the ceiling and shining down in each area. I guess this was another modern touch.

The woman said that the block was only recently built and that this apartment was brand new. She explained that it was one of the better apartments in Arkhangelsk.

I looked in the fridge. Someone had already stocked it. We had cheeses, vegetables, fruit and drinks. The woman walked over and took a bottle from the fridge.

"A small drink to celebrate," she said and poured three glasses of sekt. Mamma, Pabbi and the woman chinked their glasses together. I could tell that things had become more relaxed.

The Academy

It turned out that my arrival at The Academy was like any first day starting out. A new school and a new term. All normal. What I wasn't expecting was that there would be so much English spoken. I was taken into see the Principal. Professor Kuznetsov. He introduced himself and explained that the Academy taught a broad range of disciplines. Well beyond the normal range for a school or college. He called it the Dominion Academy a few times.

He explained that the Dominion helped keep the world in proper order. They were known for delivering justice into unjust situations, showing mercy toward human beings, and helping those in lower ranks stay organised and perform their work well.

I'll be honest. I could see a problem with this. How could I tell what was the right thing to do? Kuznetsov explained that the rest of the holistic instruction would help make this clear. He spoke mainly in English, but dropped into Russian for a few of the key terms. He said

I'd soon pick up Russian language alongside my Icelandic and English.

Once the brain had been woken to languages, especially in the young, then adding a new language should be a matter of patience.

надеюсь, что это так - I hope so.

So now I was subjected to the regime of the Academy. I was told to think of the other pupils as brothers and sisters. The Academy was outside of the town, and for the first few weeks I caught the bus from outside of the apartment. It stopped at the end of the drive leading to the Academy and usually a few pupils got off and we walked in together.

One of my friends there, Mila, told me that most people only came on the bus for a few weeks, but then moved into the Academy. They had dormitories there and usually the parents could get a special grant via the Academy for the student to stay on campus.

I could qualify under various schemes, probably including being an international or out-of-town student. Mila told me that in most cases from 2 to 4 students share a room, but if I liked I could apply with her and we could try to get a 2-person room. In a typical room there would be writing desks, chairs, closets, bookshelves, beds and nightstands. The Academy would have shared kitchens, gyms, recreation rooms, canteens, and laundromats. There are also locker rooms and bicycle sheds available. A security service operates on the premises.

I knew I was probably a little young for this, but I'd been used to doing my own cooking and laundry back at the farm in Iceland, so none of it held any fear for me. I'd miss my parents, but secretly I thought it would be a much quicker way to learn the language and become integrated with the others.

I was soon mixed in with the others, had some friends and we'd help one another out with the school work, which seemed to consist of a lot of teaching about military exploits of Russia and criticising the Americans. I couldn't help think the way America was described was very different from how I'd seen before.

Dormitory with insults

We agreed at home that I could start at the dormitory from the next term. Mamma and Pabbi were sad to see me go, but I would be back every weekend and during the breaks from studies. It was also only a bus ride away and Pabbi said he'd been given a full grant for my accommodation.

I was right as well. It helped speed up my language skills and also helped me make friends. Even after a couple of weeks, Mamma said she noticed how much more I was speaking Russian.

I didn't realise it but I was picking up the northern Russian dialect. We used to make the 'ch' sound like a 'ts', for example. I hadn't realised that there was a southern and a central dialect, with Moscow speaking the central dialect and most learned and literary types speaking the southern variant. It wasn't like some places where there were different words, just different pronunciations.

Something else about the lessons. They started early and went on for a long time. The morning was filled with learning to the head, but often the afternoon would include sport. I realised also that my time on the farm had made me very fit and that I also had good endurance.

The field sports were unusual. I had to learn archery, cross-country skiing (which was easy - I'd skied since I was tiny) and various types of rock and mountain climbing.

The instructor used to call me to the front quite regularly to demonstrate a new technique to the others. A couple of them called me *devushka fermer* or *derevenskaya devushka*, both of which meant 'farm girl', but I didn't mind. It meant I was known around the place quite quickly. Mila was a good friend to me with this though; she was Russian through and through and knew all the best insults to whip back at anyone.

Сволочь (*svolotsch'*) — The cat just dragged in this old curse word from the 14th century, and it just so happens to describe "what the cat dragged in"

Я бы вас послал, да вижу вы оттуда! (*Ya by vas paslal, da vizhu vy ottuda!*) — "I would send you there, but I see you came from there already!" Where is "there," exactly? A place only an idiot would visit.

Козёл (*kozyol*) — Calling a man a "goat" like this in Russian is a really bad form of insult and comes from old prison slang that referred to a snitch or informant.

Иди в баню! (*Idi v'banyu!*) — If you want to tell someone to get lost as dismissively as you'd swat a fly away with your hand, tell them to "go to the bathhouse."

There are a lot more, but I'm too polite to explain them.

There was one other girl in the Academy, a couple of years older than me, who understood Icelandic. Her name was Sofie, she was Norwegian, from Sunndalsøra and she spoke Norwegian, which is easy enough to understand when from Iceland.

The Academy soon split its students into different streams as they identified the strengths and weaknesses of everyone. I was put in the same group as Mila and Sofie. And that's when I began to notice a change in emphasis.

Love

"Not that she wanted to have sex with him, necessarily.

Only that she was happy to acknowledge, on this late-summer evening, that he was a man and she a woman, and if he found her attractive, that was all right with her."

— Anne Berest

Love's young dream.

Yes, the change in emphasis was because the top tier of the Academy was being fenced off for other duties. It was a subtle process, with various scheduled times that we could drop back into the more normal classes.

This Academy life spun through the years. I felt very established in the Academy. I even referred to it as the Dominion Academy. I knew we were, for all intents, being prepared to become Soviet intelligence officers.

Back in the town, my parents were quietly proud. They knew I was selected for special duties, and I think they were aware of what these were. Pabbi once saluted me, using his best, crisp Air Force salute, and I knew that he knew more than we would ever talk about. Mamma would always say how much she missed me, how I was turning into a fine young woman and attempting to give me lots of practical advice.

They had both adapted to the life and fortunately their

one-time Russian language skills had returned. They appeared to be known as 'The Farmers' although Pabbi had actually gone back into a ground role in the Air Force at a local base. Mamma seemed to be happy enough, although I thought I could see she missed the farm and the animals. She had been offered a job at the Arkhangelsk Agricultural College, to talk about running a farm, and had taken it, although the environment of the college screamed 'run-down tower-block' more than farming college.

Then I had a chance to try out some of my newly gained skills. In a class above us there was a boy named Pavel. He was like most of the boys in the higher classes. They had a manner about them which was to behave larger than life. It was a kind of machismo which seemed to be the same for many of the Russian boys and men. In Reykjavik we used to call them hnakki - A "*hnakki*" literally means "neck" and describes men, possibly from the suburbs, that are so tanned that they're orange, have highlighted or dyed hair, possibly shaved on the back and sides, go to the gym a lot and listen to bad techno music. You mostly find them at the gym, at a mall, as radio station hosts or cruising down Laugavegur in a converted car with something like Basshunter blaring from the windows.

Pavel, wasn't like that. Sofie (from her Norwegian) said he was more of a *lattelepjandi lopatrefill*. We evolved to that term, by discussing Oslo boys that hung around The Thief on Tjuvholmen and then compared them with city dwellers in Reykjavik. The term literally means "a latte-sipping woollen scarf". It's used about mostly men to describe someone who is arty, left-wing, environmentalist and who lives in 101 Reykjavik. A derogatory term applied by more conservative Icelanders who live outside of Reykjavik, and a term also popular with the *hnakkis*. Other versions include "*Lattelepjandi listamenn*,"(latte-sipping artists) and "*Lattelepjandi miðbæjarrotta*" (latte-sipping city centre rats).

Well, it didn't matter to me, Pavel was my first true love and we were seen sitting around like moody teenagers everywhere *Å leve på luft og kjærlighet* (living on air and love) as Sofie would say .

It turned out that Pavel's father worked at the *МАЛЫЕ КОРЕЛЫ* - Small Karelia, which was a museum just on the outskirts of Arkhangelsk. It was an open-air museum which featured a collection of wooden buildings reminiscent of the olden days. In the right weather it could look very picturesque and had a big car-park for tourists.

Pavel said he'd got some tickets from his dad and could take me along. I went to see it in the snowy weather, and I was surprised to see how much it reminded me of Iceland and the farm. Pavel said we should stop off at his father's office there - I don't know quite what he did - but I think it was on the administrative side. We dropped around and I was getting all ready to say thank you.

Pavel's dad seemed to know too much about me. Pavel had obviously talked! Anyway, his father made conversation by saying that he hoped we liked the place. He thought it would be even better when there were a few wild animals roaming around. He told me there were plans to have a few goats in the place, which could roam around freely.

I mentioned that we'd kept sheep on our farm, and he laughed, "I don't think your Father and Mother - A pilot and a college lecturer, would want to keep goats now!"

I said, "Don't be surprised, we all miss the farm. Even me, when I walked into the museum it reminded me of the farm and where we kept the horses and the sheep."

I was also thinking Pavel was probably obsessed with me, judging by how much he'd told his parents. This might need to be the end of my time with a *Lattelepjandi lopatrefill.*

I took the information away and as it was Saturday; I was planning to go home after the day out. Pavel and I left the museum, and he accompanied me right back to my apartment block.

I thanked Pavel for the day out and he squeezed and kissed me a bit too much. I wriggled free as the elevator arrived. Now I had interesting news for my parents. I'd need to skirt around the Pavel boyfriend part though; I don't think I'd mentioned him to them.

So I told Mamma about the museum, explained that I knew one of the people running it through a classmate, and told her the news that they were thinking about adding some livestock as a tourist attraction.

Mamma didn't initially sound that interested, but I mentioned it again over the Golubtsy, when we were eating dinner. Yes, we'd gone properly Russian at home and were eating dolma, but instead of a grape leaf – we did like the Russians and made it with cabbage leaves. Cabbage leaves stuffed with minced beef and rice. I do not need to say, that the best sauce is sour cream, right?

Pabbi looked interested in the news about the museum and said to Mamma she should look if she wanted. He knew she still missed the animals and that the repetitive lecturing to teenagers wasn't as enjoyable as her time with the land. He said he knew that a lecturer sounded higher than a land worker job, but if she was keen, then she should consider it. He said he'd also be able to spend some time there. Pabbi had received a promotion since his return and was quite a senior rank and well remunerated on the base.

Well, it went to plan. Mamma went along to the Museum, met Pavel's dad and soon had a job to obtain the goats and start them on the land at the museum. Mamma had also asked about horses and Pavel's father was interested but had said Mamma should get the goats working properly first.

So, I guess that's my first use of influence to get something; I think it showed my ruthless side too, because Pavel and I split soon after the Day Out.

I did feel slightly sorry for Pavel, when I saw him out with the hnakkis. He still looked like an outsider and I was pleased for him when he met Galinka and could go back to hanging around living on air and love.

Of course, I was getting plenty of practical advice from the Academy, not least from other students, as well as slightly artificial classes covering varied life skills. Some of these were in English too, which a few of the others struggled with, but I never had a problem thanks to Iceland's television.

The criteria were strict. We need to speak Russian. At least one other language, which was preferably English. We needed a grasp of the Western culture, maybe by having lived for some time in a western country. It was hilarious when we had a lesson on western fast food, for example.

Then we needed to be especially fit, fast and strong. We needed good practical skills and an academic ability.

They were also keen to see how well we could hunt, I remember sessions on cross-country skis with a bow and arrow, like some kind of Hunger Games Katniss Everdeen although the full implications of those sessions wasn't to occur to me for several years.

Then our schooling was taken up a notch. We were expected to understand a range of training that was reserved for FSB agents.

We needed to understand espionage, subversion and subterfuge.

Our topics included: "Psychological Methods", "Psychologically Influencing Foreigners", "Disinformation in Intelligence Materials".

They gave us computers and access to electronic manuals that covered much of this material. I thought most of it was outdated, with an apparent heritage in the 1960s to 1980s.

I was told that no less than Vladimir Putin had insisted that this tradecraft be provided to his new spies at Russia's domestic and foreign intelligence academies.

We had to practice some techniques on one another, and through this Sofie was eventually removed from our work stream- they said she didn't have a grasp for the technical stuff - but I think it was because she had a drippy cadet boyfriend messing with her studies. We were instructed to look into the documents to find lots of how-to guides, including information on "how to recruit and psychologically manipulate agents on Western soil," "how to root out enemy disinformation schemes, "how to infiltrate international scientific gatherings to recruit agents" and "how to outflank suspected agent provocateurs."

The methods had hardly changed from the true Cold War and had simply been modified to accommodate newer technologies as they came on stream. It accounts for how Russia can manipulate social media right the way through into the 2020s.

K

In my upper years at the Dominion Academy, I was schooled in KGB skills.

We were not called the KGB by then; the KGB had gone through a couple of name changes. First was the Federal Counterintelligence Service (FSK) of Russia, and then in April 1995, Russian president Boris Yeltsin had signed a law mandating a reorganisation of the FSK, which resulted in the creation of the FSB.

All the renamings didn't affect most of our papers and examples though. They were still stamped KGB and, I suppose, looked like they could have come out of the Cold War.

By 2003, the FSB's responsibilities had widened to incorporate the previously independent Border Guard Service and a major part of the abolished Federal Agency of Government Communication and Information (FAPSI).

I guess this was all political machinations behind the scenes, but didn't have much effect on the Academy, which would issue new organisation charts occasionally, but still carried on giving us old KGB Handbooks to read.

So, I was technically studying in a military academy. Under Russian federal law, the FSB is a military service just like the armed forces, the MVD, the FSO, the SVR, the FSKN, Main Directorate for Drugs Control and EMERCOM's civil defense, but its commissioned officers rarely wear military uniforms.

We were even given military ranks. Initially, I was a Kadet. I even had some epaulettes with a K to wear on special occasions. Parade Insignia looked pretty cool. Bright Red with gold stripes (of course) and a letter K.

Dominion

The upper years of the Academy were increasingly referred to as Dominion and became more focused towards the FSB training. We'd had a strong grounding in all the usual subjects. We'd all taken our *Diplom O Nepolnom Vysshem Obrazovanii* (Diploma of Incomplete Higher Education) a couple of years early. I said I thought the 'incomplete' Diploma sounded awful, but everyone said it was great to get this so young.

Then we were to study for the next level, where we would receive our Basic Higher Education. A *Bakalavr's* degree is equivalent to the Bachelors degree in the US or Western Europe.

Instead of the usual five years of studying, we were told that because we were on a compressed syllabus, we should expect to gain this after two years. And although The State Educational Standards regulate nearly 80% of curriculum content, the Academy had a special dispensation to change the syllabus.

I soon understood why. We were being given special

training for our future roles as state operatives.

As an example, one of the classes covered "intelligence operational environment".

It described the climate for agents and operatives in a given country or other setting.

We were told that, as Marxism-Leninism teaches, in order to determine the direction and forms of any activity, all the conditions for that activity must be studied.

The environment for us as agents was shaped by the political atmosphere in the country; the administrative and police regimes; geography and demography; the means of transportation; people's everyday life; the system for foreigners' residence; the means of communication and the rules and traditions for socialising, the climate and so on.

Such an environment would affect the choice of the agent's forms and methods of intelligence work.

We were told that, despite still having KGB handbooks, the intelligence climate changes constantly, influenced by politics, the economy, law, with even geography and culture having long-term effects.

The FSB also looked at what social classes there are in the country; the government's attitude toward development and the socialist countries; the presence of progressive or reactionary forces; the presence of progressive elements in the government, civic and business circles; the local population's attitude toward the government; the existence of a peace movement; and the degree to which other capitalist countries affect it.

It sounded all-embracing and not something that one person was going to be able to change.

Then we wren told that a range of factors influenced the government and everyday life including political parties, individual political figures, major monopolists of the economy; the status of science and technology; the stage of economic development.

And in a more modern vein, we should look at the various media and propaganda outlets, especially in light of the changing social impact of social media. It looked at media funding as well as the comparative population's standard of living.

So, we were looking at the scope of intelligence activities in target countries through the prism of the FSB's own communist belief system. This seemed ironic in the modern and increasingly corrupt Russia as the gangster classes were moving into the positions of influence.

The FSB could study and identify a capitalist system. The major monopolists or a conservative government hostile to the Soviet Union and/or socialism; maybe a population influenced by capitalist-controlled media distrustful of communists will all conspire to make the work of agents much harder.

I thought some of this was outdated. It was like watching a TV show in black-and-white. It accidentally emphasised the work of the new order thugs taking power in the Federation.

Another course covered "The Intelligence Officer's Agent and Operative Dictionary," Over decades of interacting with the FSB and receiving defectors from the Soviet

Union, Western intelligence agencies learned some unique terms the KGB had used to describe itself and its activities — the *rezidentura* or station in a foreign country; *konspiratsiya,* which really means "tradecraft" more than it means "conspiracy"; *razrabotka,* the "developmental" which is the art of luring recruits with a whole range of incentives and coercions, and so on.

This handbook is riddled with Marxist-Leninist ideology about class warfare and "progressive ideas" and a skewed understanding of the West.

For example, curiously, the term *oblava* or "raid" is characterised as a "specifically capitalist police activity," which is performed "especially at moments of political difficulties and during war at train stations, marketplaces, hotels, cafes, nightclubs and other public gathering places and are accompanied by the checking of documents".

It was like someone had played a couple of old movies and TV series to alien invaders and they had taken them to build their model of what everything looked like.

The FSB manual makes a distinction between an agent and a confidential contact — and the intelligence officer who is the full-time, trained employee who runs them.

I could see my destiny being pinned towards being the intelligence officer but operating with some laughably inaccurate manuals and briefings.

These sessions were easy for me, because I had so much of real life to balance the theory I was being told. I couldn't keep interrupting the instructors, so I kept my mouth shut, conscious that they were telling everyone else the wrong stories. I realised I'd need to remember these inaccuracies in order to pass the exams too.

Speaking of exams, there were some aspects that reflected the bureaucracy of Russia. Like having at least 15 types of agents - all neatly classified - and which I'd need to remember like a form of the times table.

There were the well-known agents of influence and double agents; the illegals and the tails and the informers.

Then there were the "agent identifiers" whose sole purpose is to identify people living under cover or hiding their identity under false passports. There were the "route agents" whose job is simply to follow a target on a trip abroad.

We were also supposed to learn American codes too, like "DP" (displaced person) or "G2" (the intelligence units of the US army).

And the all-important "cocktail" which is "a form of diplomatic reception".

Some terms have Western equivalents, like "safe house" and others seem specifically Soviet.

There was the KSP, *Kontrol'naya sledovaya polosa*, a 5-meter wide strip of land along the border kept regularly plowed so that the footprints of anyone attempting to escape from the Soviet Union became visible.

There are the "legals," which are the officially known intelligence officers in the *rezidentura* and the "illegals," the spies who burrow into foreign societies, sometimes spending years creating their identities, awaiting the signal to be activated.

Then there was the requirement for information gathering, so called "Information Work in Intelligence," The FSB was clear as to what motivates information work: "to reveal the enemy's secret plans and measures in a timely manner, primarily the imperialists of the United States, against the countries of the socialist alliance."

The information to be gathered includes documents on political, military, economic and scientific issues and also sketches, maps, diagrams, photos, models of technology, clandestine recordings and recordings of operatives' verbal reports.

But most of all, the FSB was interested only in secret information that would reveal enemies' secret plans and intentions. It wasn't interested in the mere recording of events, citations from the press or reports from people who didn't have access to classified information.

A lot of this dealt with physical materials, the kind of stuff one sees in the old spy movies on TV. It didn't seem to account for the move towards the Internet and data sharing. Nor, in those days did it seem to particularly interested in economically damaging information.

That all changed as Putin and the oligarchs came into power and decided that the Russian Federation could be carved up like a cake.

Another aspect was just how old some case studies were that we were given. Maybe more recent events were more sensitive, but I don't think so. They gave us case studies from the 1960s or in one case 1952, which meant we had to learn all about the prevailing climate of the time and the sometimes obscure players to understand the subterfuge that was played.

Then we had to learn about gathering Operational Backgrounders, known as sets. The "set" is a one-time operational activity involving the clandestine gathering of basic information and character references about persons or groups of interest to the FSB, and about the activity and features of the enemy's important facilities. Sometimes the set is made for the purpose of vetting information about facilities and persons.

The FSB gets these profiles to help carry out various operations, although often officers do not use them, citing them as unreliable. But then, the officers are often unreliable and don't complete the due diligence on the information supplied.

This course was interesting for the first-person narrative and variety of examples from a particular officer's experience.

When he was just starting out, he was casual and careless about preparing the profiles but then found himself in trouble when having to do them on the fly.

Despite an extensive, two-month study of public places such as museums and cafes, learning traffic rules and customs; reading local newspapers; and even striking up conversations with strangers, the agent found himself ill-prepared when he went to a foreign country.

We were given exhaustive lists of activities needed to prepare the operative who will draw up such background reports.

- study the assignment and clarify its tasks

- use official sources of information
- make a preliminary study of the target's area
- work out and document the cover legend
- preliminarily study the sources of information
- create a plan for talking to sources
- create a plan of action

When gathering information for the target's profile, there are the obvious factors such as where he went to school, whether he is married and happy in his family life and where he works but also his past residences, his close relatives, his political views, civic activities, attitude toward work, style of socialising, ways of meeting foreigners, financial status and sources of income, moral profile, recreational activities, degree of discipline, and so on.

As a cover for such detailed snooping, the FSB agent suggests pretending to be from the phone company, an insurance company, a notary/real estate office, a public opinion pollster, or a member of a society seeking supporters and donations.

I'm less convinced about the effectiveness of the last ideas, because I know when in Iceland we used to get the mobile phone companies or pollsters come around or stop us in the street, we'd just say 'No' to everything - mainly because they were usually trying to sell something.

Then there was the course on the somewhat ambitious "Mobilisation of Capitalist State Police Services in Fighting Organised Crime and Its Effect on Foreign Intelligence Activities," .

This analytical survey looks at the growth of organised

crime in the West and the related increase in police activity in the capitalist countries from the perspective of its effect on the FSB's intelligence work.

Intriguingly, it doesn't mention the equivalent increased in Mafia-like activity in Moscow, nor the huge infrastructure created to launder money and run illicit operations in Russia. It is similarly quiet about the ways that they have redistributed money from the large energy and power organisations (to name but two).

Being in the right 'wrong' club in Moscow hasn't done certain oligarchs any harm.

The course still referred to older historical events such as terrorist attacks such as on Pope John Paul II and the assassination attempt on Reagan as part of "organised crime."

Modern techniques to skew politics in varied countries including the Motherland are all missing from the course and handbook. I guess too many people could go to prison.

The course does recount the features of organised crime groups and their methods (using fake documents, transporting illegal contraband and persons, renting safe houses, etc.), which are similar to the FSB's own methods.

I thought the level of detail wasn't so different from watching an American TV show like Sopranos though - I wonder what the authors were doing writing this stuff, and I wasn't sure it would really help the next generation of agents.

The training lists the actions taken by the capitalist police forces against organised crime, along with a description of the campaign against international crime groups. A separate section describes the (so called) new technology which police were using to battle organised crime.

Police now had better methods to identify people using their photographs and fingerprints, voice prints, footprints, DNS and forensics and making use of then-new methods of hand-writing and text analysis – not to mention lie detectors.

There was some practical advice. Criminals looking for safe-houses — like the FSB — look for apartments whose windows don't face on to the windows of other apartments, which have a telephone and an elevator and an underground parking lot.

Police look for tenants who have paid in cash for several months in advance; who used fake names; who never received mail at the addresses and had mailboxes that were always empty.

None of those techniques was exactly mind-blowing, but I suppose they just needed to work.

The course went on to describe various drug cartels around the world and the top cities for drug sales and their need for buyers, sellers, loaders, transporters, etc. Drugs are often concealed in cosmetic cases; in feminine hygiene items; perfume bottles; canned food; packaging inside medication bottles; inner belts; false bottoms in shoes or suitcases, etc. Drug dealers often swallowed plastic bags as well.

Once again, most of this could just as easily be seen by watching a good movie from the right genre. Later movies explain the techniques of injection moulding the drugs to the shape of electrical goods packaging, as an example.

The course tutor complained about how the capitalist law-enforcers' stepped-up campaign against terrorism is targeting not criminals, but revolutionary and liberation movements, partisan and rebel groups who are rightfully, in the Soviet mind, fighting imperialist regimes.

The training went on to say that crime was built into the bourgeois social system itself, because there is social inequality, discrimination against minorities and other factors that push people into crime.

Ironically, the equivalent corruption in Russian society doesn't get mentioned.

Murder, smuggling, and drugs are, at the end of the day, were, the presenter said, methods of expressing dissatisfaction with the bourgeois social system.

The Soviets were critical of UN efforts to combat terrorism as they felt the definitions were vague and the means of prevention problematic.

The FSB was concerned about automated systems for population registration involving telephone numbers, rent payments, payment for gas and electric services, car registration, hotel registration, registry of radio and telephone equipment and so on which were already being done electronically, enabling authorities to amass large data bases and quickly compare them.

At German customs, it was observed, an IBM machine enabled border guards to type in a name and get three responses: "not in list," "detain" or "put under surveillance."

I wondered if the FSB was simply jealous of these more advanced countermeasures?

The next course was one I'd forever regard with scepticism. "Using Delegations and Tourism for Intelligence Purposes,"

Soviet intelligence was required to maintain "high vigilance, timely detection and interception of hostile plots and intentions of the imperialist states, above all the USA and their partners in the aggressive blocs aimed at the USSR, states friendly to us, and progressive forces."

Tourist trips abroad and other kinds of exchanges with foreigners offered an opportunity for Soviet intelligence to gather information. FSB divisions can use Soviet tourist organisations to:

- study and cultivate foreigners, above all Americans in the USSR, for the purpose of drawing them into collaboration as either agents or confidential contacts, to use them abroad in the interests of political and scientific and technical intelligence and to penetrate the enemy's intelligence services;
- to obtain intelligence political, military, scientific, technical, counterintelligence information on the USA and other imperialist countries;
- to conduct active measures and promote disinformation against the enemy;
- to bring foreigners of interest to the USSR to the USSR;
- to perform special intelligence tasks from illegal positions.

The irony here is that the FSB didn't seem to get the memo that this was an outdated tactic. Famously, even on a recent deadly mission to the UK, two Russian agents cited a cultural trip to Salisbury cathedral to see...and then quoted a word-perfect rendition of the Google description of the Cathedral.

Of course, the Cultural exchanges went both ways, with Russians abroad and tourists into Russia.

Despite the increasing prevalence, Russian brides didn't get a mention during this course. We were all waiting for it to be mentioned, but I think the presenter was embarrassed.

I suppose the nearest we got to Russian Brides, was the so-called "Dangle" technique to expose something of great interest as a hook.

In the FSB teachings, the Dangle could be a much longer-term thing, sometimes extending to many years.

A complicated example described an agent who first worked for the KGB, but then was found to be double-crossing them. The story sound more like a long and rather tired joke being told in a pub.

It involves "Albert" a furrier and wealthy Cossack who fled to Turkey, then back to Germany where he had a romance with the daughter of a German Air Force general, and opportunity via an Englishman obtaining various items like paint, window frames, door handles and carpentry tools, at discount prices to supply a construction company repairing post-war East Berlin.

Albert then switches from construction to start a business selling carpets in Germany which runs for ten years before he asked by the KGB to do anything. When he is, he is already tailed by the Germans and finally picked up by the Russians.

It smacks of a comedy that was largely uncontrolled and without purpose yet is being trotted out as a worked example in the training. No wonder "Albert" disappeared.

By now, you'll be getting the impression that this training wasn't very helpful. Well, in one way it was, it helped show many of the flaws in thinking of the average agent operative.

I'll briefly mention another technique we were shown, that of 'False-Flag Recruitment,' Because of the worsening climate for intelligence operations, the FSB had to refine its false-flag recruitments. Once again it was far too complicated to be successful, with people tripping over their own and everyone else's shoelaces.

The simple idea is to put someone in, under another country's flag, to be the advisor or assistant to someone important. The FSB way is to have more than one person doing this and then complicated hand-offs and monitoring.

Easily this can lead to some double agent moments. The most likely thing is that the agent entering into these arrangements will later be compromised and end up being either blackmailed or caught and shot, often by the very same FSB who placed him in the first place.

If I don't sound too keen on any of these schemes, it is because I think they came from an earlier age and are just unsuitable for modern thinking.

I never dreamt I would be enrolled in any of them.

Officer

Not everything assumes a name. Some things lead beyond words.

Aleksandr Isayevich Solzhenitsyn

Krasimira Radka

By now I'd been Agnes Dobrayadoch for around eight years. So, what would happen next? Yes - another new passport.

I was through the first wave of the Academy now, and they had passed me with flying colours. My mother and Father were proud because I was given a new rank. Yes, I'd be a Lieutenant now, which was a proper field officer grade. OF-1. There was a ceremony for all of this, and my father gave me another one of his proper salutes. Mamma asked me to look after myself.

The ceremony was also the time when I was told about my first official posting. They wanted to send me abroad, but to somewhere that I could learn about military hardware. This was getting to be a long way from sheep, horses, piano playing and singing.

The Russians gave me another new passport. This one was Bulgarian. They said I would go to Bulgaria, to another Military Academy, to learn about weapons. It was The Vasil Levski National Military University and was right in the middle of Bulgaria.

The first time went there I'd say it was closer to Bucharest in Romania than it was to Sofia in Bulgaria and it was also over 200 twisty kilometres from Plovdiv, the main airport.

I'd had to fly from Arkhangelsk to Moscow and then change planes to one to Plovdiv International, in Bulgaria. Then an army truck picked me up to take me on the last part of the journey, which was some 3,600 kilometres in all, from the cold of Arkhangelsk to the heat of middle Bulgaria. Sitting in the back of the truck, Bulgaria looked poor. There were farmers scratching a living, but they seemed to be using horses and carts to get around. Several of the towns we passed through still had giant statues of one-time Communist party leaders.

I arrived at Vasil Levski under the name Krasimira Radka, a Bulgarian national who had spent her whole life in Russia. This time, they didn't give me a proper back-story, so I made one up about living on a small farm in Russia. I just transposed all of my time in Iceland, which meant it was easy to have good anecdotes. I must have learned that in the Academy.

"Here we go again," I thought, as I realised that Bulgarian language may look similar to Russian, but it is completely different. I could read most signs and notices and understand about 80%, but I didn't have the right grammar to start talking to anyone. Luckily there were three of us transferred to Vasil Levski and so I had a couple of other Russian accomplices while we got to know our way around. The other two had not been given backstories either, and all three of us had new names, which were difficult to remember, when we knew each other from the Academy, with our original Russian names.

I decided that this was also a part of the training, to be placed in a foreign country with an alias and to then get along.

Most of the others at the Bulgarian Academy were also Bulgarian, although there were a few other nationalities mixed in. The true Bulgarians made some fun about us, saying that we were pretend-Bulgarians. They seemed to know about the Russians placing people in the Academy. They had a nickname for us - *Kifla* - which meant loaves but was their slang for selfie models. It implied that we were there to get selfies of ourselves standing by Bulgarian scenes.

We decided it was best not to have a slang for the Bulgarians, because it would only escalate. Andrei Raikov and Aneta Yanev were my accomplices during this time. We were all Russian, but when we chatted, we discovered that we'd all been somewhere else before the Russian Federation. Andrei had been in Finland and Aneta had been in Sweden. We began to see the picture developing.

Now this Bulgarian Academy was much more about Boys and their Toys than the Archangel Academy. My impression of Bulgaria was of an old-fashioned version of Russia. They spoke in an old-fashioned Slavic style and there were greater remnants of the Communist era left in the streets. But they knew how to set up a modern military academy!

We had everything, firearms, rifles, anti-tank, anti-aircraft, actual tanks. Both Russian and American. I was told that Bulgaria had skilfully played the NATO game and been given hardware by just about every country. No wonder it was such a good place to train. There were fields to play war games and laughably, if the weather was bad, there were also indoor shooting ranges.

I think I learned just about every type of weapon and also got a reputation as an excellent shot, and gun handler, which I reckon was because of my prior time on the farm.

The instructors all said my field skills were almost instinctive and several of the other class-mates grudgingly admitted that this *Kifla* was actually pretty good. One day Andrei, Aneta and I took our camera phones to the class and posed in front of a few tanks and other weapons for a few selfies. It only took a moment and there was a scramble from the rest of the class to be in the pictures. Even the instructor!

And that's when we seemed to get accepted into the rest of the gang. They still laughed at our Bulgarian - why do some words even get spelled the same but have different meanings? - And they accepted our flimsy stories about our past.

The year passed quickly, and I was soon on my way back to Arkhangelsk. By then, I would miss some of my classmates and the mild weather and I knew that when I got back home, they would probably give me yet another identity before releasing me for work.

PART TWO

Operative

*"Wear a black bra under your white blouse,
like two notes on a sheet of music."*

— Caroline de Maigret

Katarina Voronin

Well, I was right. I returned to Arkhangelsk to yet another promotion. I somehow jumped from one star to - wait for it - four stars on my epaulettes. They had made me up to Captain. It was a little unbelievable, but they explained that when I was a field officer on a mission, the grade was needed to ensure that other people did as they were asked.

I'd never really thought about the degree that I'd be dealing with the silent Russian bureaucracy until this moment, so anything that could help would be useful. On my dress uniform, the stars were arranged in a kind of arrow formation and now I had so much gold that the red stripe had almost turned into a line.

In all modesty though, I realised that the actual grades I'd gone through were OF-D, OF-1 and now OF-2.

When I returned, and we had the Defence of the Fatherland Day ceremony, I realised that I'd jumped much higher than some of my compatriots, some of whom still had their red epaulettes with the letter 'K'. They had to salute me now, which we all thought was hilarious.

Needless to say, Pabbi and Mamma were still as proud as anything of me, although Pabbi didn't salute me this time but instead hugged me and said I should be careful. Mamma looked at me with a tear in her eye as if she couldn't believe that I'd made it to this grade.

To top it all, I was awarded a PhD from the NMU in Bulgaria. The National Military University had looked at my work and it had been deemed good enough for the Ph.D. I was told by my instructors back in the Archangel Academy that one of the aspects of a good officer was that they had both rank and qualification. In practice, the Ph.D was window-dressing for my role.

Now my Passport was once again Russian. I was called Katarina Voronin, and the passport came with its own back-story. It looked as if I'd already travelled to several countries, judging by the stamps in it.

I was told that I'd be sent on some missions to various countries to interfere with their smooth running. At first glance, this looked as if it was quite evil. But I'd been through the training and belief system of the Russian State. A first and most important implication is the belief among Russian soldiers that their country is already at war.

Some in the West want to draw a clear distinction between war and peace. The current Kremlin leadership does not see this divide. The message it has portrayed over the past several years is that Russia has been engaged in a defensive "war" against the West/United States, which remains intent upon preventing Russia from regaining its superpower status.

Using economic, information, diplomatic, and other means, the Russian soldiers believe that their country has already been "attacked" by the West/United States. Having repeatedly been taught that Russia is engaged in a defensive struggle against U.S./Western aggression, they honestly believe that theirs is a just struggle and that truth and righteousness are on the Russian side.

The prevalent mood in Soviet society after World War II could be summed up as "do everything possible to avoid another war." That generation had experienced the full horror of modern conflict, and even after the USSR attained superpower status, Soviet society understood that war should be avoided at all costs.

Nowadays, this sentiment may no longer be prevalent, particularly among the younger generation, who have been taught that war is a viable option.

Believing that their country is now under threat from the United States, young Russians are increasingly prepared to take up arms to fight against the "enemy."

I was told that my missions would be secret and that I would be denied if I was caught. Of course, the military gave me a good pay cheque every month because I was a Russian field officer, but I could not admit to the rank if I was detained. Only if I was working with other Russians and needed a command structure.

As Katarina Voronin, I did dozens of missions. Sometimes I needed a weapon, other times not. It was mainly work of a security nature. The thinking seemed to be that the men from the Academy would handle the offensive work and leave the defensive and security work to the women.

My first missions were mainly of a security nature. As an example, the Russian State was using money supplied by oligarchs to influence trade deals. I was along to ensure there was no tricky business during the summits. In the jargon I was a 'gun girl' sent into a 'pay-to-play' deal. What this meant was that some high-ranking official, maybe from the United States, was offered money - a lot of money - to help foster an advantageous trade deal for Russia.

The setup was straightforward enough. The politician or western influencer would set up a Foundation with a seemingly innocuous title. Either just their name or some kind of children's or health charity. Then the influencer would deposit a large donation. Maybe a million dollars, or more, into the Foundation.

An example was a Royal who "donated" $12 million to a Foundation in return for a meeting with a very senior politician. It later resulted in a $157 million weapons deal for an African monarchy. Pay to play.

In another example, a different senior politician accepted a $1 million check as a "birthday present" from an Arab state. The generous "gift" was followed by a 1,400 percent increase in arms sales to that Arab state, in a deal signed off on by the politician-run State Department. Oh yes, you'd recognise the name too.

I had to attend these meetings, in plain clothes carrying concealed weapons. It was to insure against trickery, double-cross, or maybe a scam from some kind of media hack trying to capture something untoward on camera.

I came to realise that the real ruling class in America are the largely Russian oligarchs. Putin's Puppet may be a moniker for the President, but it is surprisingly accurate too.

And I should mention the well-known case too, of a company called "Uranium One" which was sold to Russian government-controlled interests, giving Russia effective control of one-fifth of all uranium production capacity in the United States.

I was in the room during the negotiations, running protection for the Russian negotiator, one of whom had a sleazy penchant for women protectors. Since uranium is considered a strategic asset, with implications for the production of nuclear weapons, the deal had to be approved by a committee composed of representatives from a number of US government agencies.

Among the agencies that eventually signed off the deal was the State Department.

The Committee on Foreign Investment in the United States (CFIUS) comprises, among others, the secretaries of the Treasury, Defence, Homeland Security, Commerce and Energy.

As Russian interests gradually took control of Uranium One, millions of dollars were donated to a well-known Foundation between 2009 and 2013 from individuals directly connected to the deal including the Chairman of Uranium One.

I had to attend around a dozen sessions, spread all over the world, including on a huge Russian yacht in the Mediterranean. The sleazy negotiator had insisted that the female crew members wear sailor outfits for that one. I didn't, claiming that I needed my clothes to conceal the weapons.

Mysteriously these contributions from the Chairman of Uranium One were not publicly disclosed. Some of those papers disclosed by Julian Assange in the Podesto Papers, appear to make reference to this set-up, as does the New York Times from the era.

There were plenty of other sessions as a part of a security detail. I wasn't dressed up in a black business suit, nor did I have a curly wire headset and dark glasses, like some typical TV bodyguard. Sometimes the macho guys would think I was part of the laid-on entertainment, but I had various moves to handle that, the most extreme of which involved an ice bucket and elevated my status within the protection community.

Being Russian, that quickly got changed to an ice pick in the rumours.

I told everyone that my signature item of clothing was a pistol. And because I'd been trained at the Academy, I was increasingly referred to by my callsign Archangel-1.

Triple Threat

Now that's when things got complicated. I mentioned that my passport had other stamps in it. What I didn't realise is that Russia was operating three separate Katarina Voronins. We all had similar looks, so were getting consistently identified by any eyewitnesses. The problem was that the other two Katarina Voronins were involved in more hideous crimes.

I was mainly running protection, whereas they were out on assassinations and some forms of terrorism.

It was when I was pulled in by the British as the result of a small assignment to London, that I realised this. The questioner was fairly low-level and probably gave away more than he should have done. It was the first alert to me that Voronin was being used as a blanket cover-name for different people.

I was accused of a bombing in Amsterdam. Some kind of market square had been blown up, with civilian casualties. I was even shown pictures. I realised immediately that I was not even in Europe at the time this occurred. I had been detailed to go to San Jose in California and was running a security operation in the

San Jose Fairmont on the date and time of the explosion. It didn't take long to get proof of this, although I was concerned that it could interfere with another mission.

In San Jose, the Russians were attempting to buy a source code for an anti-virus package, stolen from a well-known American software house. Fortunately, I could keep most of what was happening secret from SI6 during their questioning of me. It was interesting to see how quickly they let me go when they realised there was no case to answer on the Netherlands situation. If that had been Russian interrogation, they'd have left me on the hook for a whole lot longer in case I blabbed about something else.

But what I also gained from the SI6 questioner, was that they had an inconsistency in their tracking of Katarina Voronin. She was alleged to have been in Istanbul at the same time as Amsterdam. I realised at once that it was different people, but I'm not sure that the Brits ever cottoned on to it.

I also wondered if the other Katarinas had ever been in a similar situation and realised that there was more than one of us.

Better than Kifla

I didn't mind being called Archangel. For a start, it was better than *Kifla*, which I'd been called in Bulgaria. And I was getting so used to the constant name changes now, although I sometimes didn't look up when someone called for 'Katarina'.

Michael as an Archangel was Arkhangelsk's official Saint. He becomes featured in many of the major religions and is described as leading armies against Satan's forces in the Book of Revelation, where during the war in heaven he defeats Satan. Catholic sanctuaries to Michael appeared in the 4th century, when he was first seen as a healing angel, and then over time as a protector and the leader of the army against the forces of evil.

Most of the depictions, including those on the flag of Arkhangelsk, showed the Archangel defeating Satan, sometimes shown as a person and other times as a black shadow.

And that's sometimes how I thought that America was portrayed to the Russians. Forget the homely television programs I watched in Iceland. Friends, Malcolm in the Middle, 3rd Rock from the Sun. Instead, think of America like that black shadow on the flag.

The United States has been portrayed unremittingly in the Russian media as the primary source of much of the world's instability.

According to Kremlin-sponsored pundits, the United States deliberately sows unrest (often under the guise of liberal democracy promotion) to maintain its global hegemony. There's been several movies about this very act and it often features in the back-stories of American TV heroes.

At the end of the Cold War, the United States assumed the role of the "indispensable nation," disregarding the global security structures built after World War II. It was an early manifestation of America First, set to play out again in the 21st Century.

According to Russian commentators, because the United States controls the global money supply, Washington has been able to convert its economic advantage into sheer military power.

The Kremlin leadership often points out the wide discrepancy between how much the United States spends on the military compared to the rest of the world.

A key theme within much of the Russian information space is the belief that given their long history of repelling foreign invaders, Russia has experience, wisdom, and truth on their side.

The Russian media have portrayed U.S. operations in Iraq, Afghanistan, Libya, Syria, and elsewhere largely as failures, where the United States has only exacerbated problems in these countries.

Every botched American operation, every errant missile strike, every case of torture or criminality perpetrated by U.S. military members, and every scandal or leak that reflects poorly on U.S. Armed Forces receives the widest possible exposure within the Russian media. Putin and The Kremlin's narrative highlights both the lack of a comprehensive military strategy and what they consider as the hypocrisy of promoting American democracy via military power.

The American military is portrayed as being over concerned with safety and political correctness, while being soft and dependent upon a huge logistical tail.

The American soldier is depicted as unwilling to fight if he or she is not supplied with all the comforts of home, right down to the GI MacBurger.

At the official level, Russia remains a very traditional, conservative country, whose population regards gender equality and gay rights as both weak and decadent. We women trainees from the Academy had to take a lot of shit on the way through. It was satisfying to have four stars on my epaulettes and to look into the faces of some of those original *muzhestvennost'* boys.

The same sentiments led to the Russians coining a derogatory slang term for American soldiers, *"пиндосы"* [pindosy], using it to mock and belittle Americans in uniform. Pindosy became associated with stupid and ill-bred, yet cunning and dangerous people (and it was also a bit reminiscent of several Russian curse words). I'll stick to being called the far less offensive *Kifla*.

The superiority of Russian weapon systems is also a popular topic within the Russian media. Russian media are constantly claiming that Russian modern, conventional weapon systems "have no analogy in the West."

I'll reserve judgement there. I know when I was in Bulgaria, the US-made pistols and other weapons certainly felt more precise than some of the jangling Russian ironmongery they gave me. The AK-47 was the exception to this. Maybe it was made from old tractors, but it was entirely dependable. Of course, US-made rifles shot straight, although were not a match for some precision UN-supplied Swiss weapons.

The same braggadocio about supremacy exists in the nuclear realm. Over the past few years, the Russian media have repeatedly reminded their audience of the country's ability to transform the United States into a parking lot or as the head of Rossiya Segodnya news agency Dmitry Kiselyov put it, 'radioactive dust.'

Based upon Chernobyl, I'm less sure. We in Russia may be able to make the whole world into a parking lot. I'm less convinced we could do so selectively or without a lot of paperwork.

I don't usually wear my uniform, but I see a lot of young Russians now wearing military uniforms and prepared to challenge U.S. claims of dominance. Up to the highest levels, Russian military personnel may have fallen victim to believing their own propaganda as to the superiority of their military power.

All of this sabre rattling by the Russian army is great bait for US presidents. They wait to be goaded and to be able to show some position of strength.

The U.S. military has already begun to recalibrate and

adjust to an increased threat from the Russian military and the Kremlin's associated information operations.

This increased focus on measures to thwart possible Russian aggression needs to be balanced by both an awareness of escalatory dangers and a willingness to cooperate where security interests align.

But where Americans might refer in Newspeak terms to 'democracy promotion' or 'concern for human rights,' a Russian would see naked aggression or geopolitical manoeuvring.

U.S. military personnel should understand that their Russian counterparts question U.S. claims of global dominance and will not be intimidated by threats of 'shock and awe.' Nor by the comedic posturing of an idiot nominally put in charge.

Given the Kremlin's indirect control over the major Russian media, they could be directed to adopt a more balanced and objective approach toward today's 'enemy.'

Nevertheless, despite economic challenges, there are currently no signs that the Kremlin leadership has modified its strategic objectives of weakening the United States and NATO. The American leadership is making much of this easy for Russia. Quite contrary to the prevailing climate, the oddly erratic current US-leadership is also challenging the NATO alliance.

Now that's the world that Katarina Voronin (and her two shadows) has to negotiate.

Assignments

And I wonder when I'll be home again
and the morning answers "Never"
And the evening sighs,
and the steely Russian skies go on
forever

Al Stewart

Krasnaya devitsa

After the time I was hauled in front of SI6, I was sent off on various other missions around Europe, maybe a dozen to twenty per year. I knew, now, that there were other copies of me running around, and I wondered if it would be possible to make contact.

I had to listen out on the varied news feeds for signs of what an agent like me would do. I also tried the social media sites, but after one incident they almost dried-up completely. A wave of cadets from one of the central Moscow Military Academies had all reached their passing out time. They foolishly celebrated by hiring a dozen big black Hum-Vees and driving them around Moscow in formation, while playing loud music. They also took both selfies and video footage of the occasion and then, with the stupidest of ideas, added a music track and posted it to YouTube. Very handy to help the west identify this group of budding agents.

The hierarchy went ballistic about this and pulled in the culprits. I'm not sure if any of them have been posted yet, or whether they are all still scrubbing floors in the Academy.

Because of this and a few other indiscretions, information gleaned from social media sites used by Russian military personnel has largely dried up.

There are still several other sources that can be exploited to gauge what military personnel are thinking. Besides the sites sponsored by the Russian Ministry of Defence (e.g., *Zvezda* TV and *Krasnaya Zvezda* newspaper), there are military-themed programs on major Russian media, as well as websites, blogs, and publications that reflect current Russian military thinking.

The Komsomolskaya Pravda Radio program, *Voennoye Review* (Military Review), provides a good example of current Russian military attitudes.

This hour-long program airs nationwide, Monday through Friday, and is hosted by two retired Russian army colonels, Viktor Baranets and Mikhail Tymoshenko (As cadets, we called it the Vik and Mik show)

It usually comprises a short introduction on a military-related topic with the rest of the program devoted to answering questions from the call-in audience. It's an example of 'only in Russia' really.

Occasionally, they will host senior military personnel who will also answer questions from a phone-in audience. As they record this program live, it often captures the raw sentiments of both the hosts and the audience.

Unlike most official Russian sources, the colonels Baranets and Tymoshenko have no problem expressing their open disdain and scorn toward the United States and its military.

Not only do they constantly repeat the Kremlin's assertion that Washington is intent upon preventing Russia from recovering its superpower status, but, in nearly every episode, they also find grounds to disparage how the United States conducts military operations.

There is likely a generation factor among Russian military personnel and how they view the American military. The older generation who were influenced by Soviet propaganda may be more inclined to embrace the current Kremlin rhetoric. Even though some of these more senior military personnel may see through the current Kremlin propaganda, to speak out could have negative career consequences.

And then younger military members have been exposed to the same anti-American, patriotic onslaught of past decade, but they may be more proficient in relying upon other, less tendentious media sources.

None of this filled me with hope, nor did it bode well for the next layer of administration to arrive in the FSB. Young guns with flippant attitudes, brain conditioned by the old guard. I decided that we Voronins were an endangered species.

Vzyatki (bribes)

The mission that tipped the scales for me was another protection one. This time it was the Russian Prime Minister who was involved in a meeting with a US administration representative. Russia was setting up sanctions and wanted the US to play along. A particular US businessman (guess who?) was in opposition because of a large deal he was about to fulfil.

Anyway, after the angry meeting, the Prime minister put up on his Facebook page that, "Any hopes of improving Russian relations with the new US administration are dead, that the current administration demonstrated complete impotence by transferring executive power to Congress 'in the most humiliating manner', and most notably, that the US just declared a full-scale trade war on Russia."

The signing of new sanctions against Russia into law by the US president leads to several consequences. First, any hope of improving our relations with the new US administration is over. Second, the US just declared a full-scale trade war on Russia. Third, the Administration showed it is utterly powerless, and in the most humiliating manner transferred executive powers to Congress. This shifts the alignment of forces in US political circles.

What does this mean for the U.S.? The American establishment completely outplayed the President. The President is not happy with the new sanctions, but he could not avoid signing the new law. The purpose of the new sanctions was to put the President in his place. Their ultimate goal is to remove the President from power. An incompetent player must be eliminated or at least positioned advantageously.

At the same time, the interests of American businesses were almost ignored. Politics rose above the pragmatic approach. Anti-Russian hysteria has turned into a key part of not only foreign (as has been the case many times) but also domestic US policy.

What does this mean for Russia? Russia will continue to work on the development of the economy and social sphere, deal with import substitution, solve the most important state tasks, counting primarily on themselves. Russia has learned to do this in recent years.

Within almost closed financial markets, foreign creditors and investors will be afraid to invest in Russia due to worries of sanctions against third parties and countries. In some ways, it could benefit Russia, although sanctions - in general - are meaningless.

Separately, Russia's foreign minister indicates that Russia retains the right to impose new countermeasures, adding the US sanctions are short-sighted, and risk harming global stability. He concludes that and attempts to pressure Russia will not make it change course.

The Kremlin also chose not to escalate the situation further. "This changes nothing. There is nothing new here," Vladimir Putin's press secretary, Dmitry Peskov, told the media in Moscow. "Counter-measures have already been taken."

From my protection perspective, I could see that the wheels were in motion to use soft power to manipulate the situation. The Russian click-farms were primed. There would be a massive manipulation of the American public over a sustained period.

No-one needs to know that this is happening and by its very stealth it could prove immensely effective. The Americans in the negotiation took another view. They simply wanted to lash out. Sanctions, Oil Pricing, Currency, Threats. It was in a downward spiral, and the pilot had lost control of the plane.

Alya Sokolov

Oh yes, the countermeasures were taken by the Putin administration. They were busy setting up click-farms around Russia and one was coming to Arkhangelsk. A click-farm was a large group of workers hired to click on paid advertising links, like, share, comment, subscribe, follow, or leave reviews for any social media page or account. It is click fraud that helps companies and individuals gain online influence.

Russia latched on to this for manipulating elections and stirring politics, long before it became popular with other socially engineered aspects of the Internet.

Click-farms are an example of astroturfing, which is a term used to describe online activity where people generate the impression that something is real, while it is fake. It is about generating likes, comments, views, etcetera to manufacture an impression of popularity.

People may use it to sell carpet cleaners or to put the next politician in power.

The click-farm in Arkhangelsk was in a building that looked almost identical to the Agricultural college where Mamma had worked, before she moved to the open-air museum.

For just a few dollars, people can purchase thousands of clicks, for example in the form of 'likes'. These clicks, this simulated traffic, is difficult to filter as fake because the visitor behaviour of the farms appears the same as that of an actual legitimate visitor.

In influence strategy, there's the popularity principle. "The more contacts you have and make, the more valuable you become, because more people think you are popular and hence want to connect with you'.

In other words, more engagement means more visibility.

I saw this as a decay of values. I was supposed to run security for people managing this click-farm, which was, itself, trying to make certain items popular at the expense of others.

The sales pitch went that buying followers or likes does not break any laws, but the practice is generally discouraged by social media companies. Social media platforms try to detect the work of click-farms, but have difficulty doing so.

In general, buying fake likes or followers is legal, but social media companies are constantly working on detecting the fake activities, and there is a chance the online marketing loses its viability if you rely on fake activity in boosting your visibility. Not so to a Russian.

Whether click-farms are legal is a different story. There are no government regulations that render them illegal but click-farms do breach a number of laws.

For example, Thai police discovered a massive click-farm in Bangkok and arrested the three Chinese owners. The perpetrators used about 500 smartphones and 350,000 SIM cards to sell views and likes for the Chinese messaging app WeChat. Three men were charged with working without a permit and importing phones without paying taxes. The fraud is punishable under law in China, and the choice to operate in Bangkok may have to do with China allowing only one phone linked to a WeChat account in to prevent fraud.

When I was running a security assignment, I went inside a click-farm. It looked like miserable work, sitting at screens in dingy rooms facing a blank wall, with windows covered by bars, and sometimes working through the night.

Click-farms operate in the dark - literally and figuratively and the working places are usually dark rooms without any daylight or windows for fresh air.

Since click-farms want to be active 24 hours a day, most click-farmers work in a three-shift system. But that system is not always followed, and most farmers work around 12 hours a day. This means that click-farmers spend long hours in dark places behind a screen.

Each click-farm generates thousands of fake accounts with fake emails, and for the names of these accounts they use a random name generator.

For just a few dollars, people can buy thousands of clicks. The reason people want to buy these clicks is because in our current media environment, social media are important spaces for creating trends, for being visible and gaining audiences. Besides that, social media influences what is visible in 'traditional' media as well, which further encourages the use of click-farms to generate visibility for oneself or one's cause.

In Putin's Russia, these click-farms were a way to buy approval. A way to tilt the game without other bloodshed.

After all the training in the Academy and spread over other countries, I could see my role being changed by the recent technology and the influence strategies of robot telephones.

So I quit.

I'd been training, or active in the FSB for half of my life. I'd run dozens of successful missions, with no blow-back. They tried to dissuade me but could see that my mind was made up. They told me about Katarina Voronin and her multiple roles and that I would therefore need another new identity.

I had to pretend to not know about Katarina.

I soon became Alya Sokolov, a freelance agent, complete with full passports and other documentation, provided by the very grateful Academy, along with an immediate retainer income, which was pitched at the same level as my enhanced military salary. They said they'd also give me the permanent agent name of Archangel, and that in return for their release of me, they would prefer to stay in touch.

I knew what this meant. Live my own life but be an agent

capable of reactivation. I realised they had all of us agents on a conveyor belt. I'd just reached the next stage.

I told my parents that I was financially secure. Mamma was mightily relieved and said she hoped I'd return home to the apartment. Pabbi could see that I'd grown past it and was now wanting a free life, away from the parents. He understood. He hugged me and did one more of his best salutes.

We both knew that it would probably be the last one from him, as I became a civilian again.

Free will

Болтуна язык до добра не доведёт.

The tongue will bring the chatterer no good.

Russian Proverb

Freelance

I'd had good pay from the FSB and they also provided me with an ongoing retention fee. I soon realised that I'd need some additional income if I was to live outside of Russia. It meant I didn't need to work particularly long hours, so I kept my fee rate card set high.

I was still offered work and I think my multiple languages, cultures and hands-on use of so many weapons meant I was always in demand. I used my new name, Alya Sokolov, but became known by my code-name of Archangel. I didn't promote the latter, but it just seemed to follow me around.

I thought it helpful because it added to my status and had a superhero ring to it as well. It was kinda cool. I learned from other freelancers that it was best to get paid in hard currencies too.

I needed to base myself somewhere and initially thought of London, where I'd been asked to operate on several occasions. Then I was contacted by one of my girl friends from Archangel, who happened to live in Paris. Her name was Galina Nabrovsky, and we'd been an item in Archangel. She'd just returned to Europe from the USA. An ice skater; she did the freelance security work alongside it. Being a skater, she was also super-fit. She suggested that we should get an apartment together in Paris. It was in the 6th Arrondissement and close to Saint-Germain-des-Prés and Mabillon on the Metro. We were hidden in the bohemian part of Paris and could walk to Châtelet in a few minutes to get a metro to any part of Paris.

We both knew the situation as we moved in together and could look out for one another. Galina was already part of the LGBT scene in Paris and her friends were often a little wild when they came to visit. I didn't know so many people in Paris to begin with, and had to learn the language, although my Slavic-sounding Russian and my English attracted its own followers.

The amusement of our frequent visitors was that both of us seemed to travel extensively. We were often on assignments, and in Galina's case she explained it away as being competitions or trials for her skating. I didn't have any good excuses for my travel and thought at one stage of saying I was a photographer. I ran into an immediate problem with this because it was a practical skill that others wanted to use. Instead I re-awoke my singing and guitar playing and said I was also a musician.

That gave me the reason to travel, although people in Paris were also pressuring me to sing for them.

I knew I'd be cornered one day and quietly acquired a guitar to practice some songs. I mainly knew Russian and Icelandic folk songs and at home in Arkhangelsk I'd played these on a Balalaika. That's right, a three stringed instrument where two of the strings are tuned the same. It would take me some time to get competent with the guitar.

I started out playing *Krassnyi Sarafan* (The red Sarafan), *Kalakoltschik* (The little bell) and *Maja Galobuscka* (My little dove). Galina said I should learn to play Kalinka too, but she kindly got me a Beatles Made Easy song book from Shakespeare and Company on the rue Dupuytren. It also gave me the excuse to sing in English instead of Russian. And to be honest, I didn't have to play so fast as with some of those Balalaika tunes.

For the assignments, we both shared a handler. His name was Theo, and he was Belgian and said he was from Brussels, but we were never really sure. He could speak French and English but seemed to blank out if we spoke to one another in Russian. Most of his missions for us were security-related. Nothing particularly dangerous, and I think he underestimated our capabilities. Still, the money was good, and it was also cash, so we didn't complain too much.

One day, a massive parcel arrived for Galina, which we opened together in the kitchen. She hadn't expected it, and when we did finally open it, we both took a step back.

"It's a 511," said Galina. "A Swiss Arms 511 sniper rifle."

"Er - DID you order it?" I asked, rather stupidly.

"No - you can't exactly buy these on Amazon," she answered.

"Someone is sending this to me for a job," she said.

We looked at it some more. Many kilos of black metal, packed small into a shipping box, but unfolding to make a deadly weapon capable of firing a huge bullet up to three kilometres.

The instructions in the box were in German. It explained that this was the 600 mm barrel version and weighed around 13 kilos. The magazine could hold 5 shots and there were two mags in the container, along with a box of .50 bullets, which looked more like shells.

'Präzise, kraftvoll ist die SAN 511 für leicht gepanzerte Ziele, bis zu 3.000 m, einsetzbar!' said the marketing spiel.- 'Precise, powerful, the SAN 511 can be used for lightly armoured targets, up to 3,000 m!'

We looked at one another. Galina was fit and powerful, but I wondered if she could even carry the weight of the fully assembled weapon, let alone use it.

"There must be someone they really dislike," said Galina, looking at the unexpected delivery.

"Have you used one before?" I asked, thinking about the practicalities.

"Yes, I've used an OM50," said Galina, "They were like the predecessors of these. It doesn't look so very different."

"Yes, what were they called? The Nemesis!" I remembered.

"It's one thing to have the rifle delivered here, but quite another to use it," said Galina, "I'd need to get out on some land and trial it, calibrate it, that sort of thing. It's tougher to do that in the heart of Paris than it was in the fields around Archangel."

I looked at Galina. I realised she wasn't as proficient with weapons as me. I spoke before I could check myself, "I'll come along and help, if you like," I said.

I have never seen Galina look so relieved.

"Would you? Mon cher'" she smiled, "I'll have to bring the car around to the apartment."

We looked at the packaging. Contained within, there was a large-sized box to carry the dissembled weapon. We'd have to carry it downstairs and into the car without attracting attention.

The box screamed Dangerous Black Gun Box from every angle. We'd need to revise it somehow.

"I know," I said, "We can flaunt it as something to do with my act."

The next afternoon, we were out at Rue de la Roquette, in Brico Corner, buying spray paint.

"Pink?" asked Galina. I nodded, "And maybe something else eye catching?"

"Purple? Asked Galina.

I nodded again. We'd make the case into a part of a stage act.

"We still haven't heard from anyone about this, " said Galina.

"He'll be along," I said, referring to Theo.

That's when Galina's phone rang.

"Hi," she answered, she nodded toward me and mouthed, "Theo"

"...Yes, I have,"

"...I'll need more information,"

"...When?"

"...Where?"

"...Ok, at seven,"

She put the phone down.

"Theo's coming to the cafe tonight, seven o'clock. He says he'll explain everything. Can you come along?" she looked at me.

"Sure, I'll come," I was thinking about what I was getting into, but also that I wasn't sure Galina could handle it on her own.

There was also the factor that Theo was a slightly creepy and usually sounded intoxicated.

We made our way to Café de Flore to be there for 7 pm. It was as busy as usual. A mix of locals and tourists on some kind of literary pilgrimage. We took two chairs and a small table outside on the pavement. We both wore sunglasses to help us people watch in case Theo was late.

"deux cafés s'il vous pla"t et une bouteille d'eau," asked Galina.

The waiter smiled and was away. Then a voice to the waiter..."Préparez ces trois cafés, s'il vous pla"t," It was Theo - he'd ordered himself a coffee too and was bringing over a chair to join us. He kissed us on both cheeks, but I thought he held both of us just a little too long. I could tell he'd been drinking.

"So, you received the item?" asked Theo.

"Yes, thank you, but we'll need to be told the purpose," said Galina.

"This is a simple one really, "said Theo, "Your role is to stop a car on the edge of the Seine. It needs to stop at a precise point, so your role is to, " he lowered his voice, " shoot out the engine with the provided weapon."

"Okay," said Galina, "But from what distance?"

"Across the river on the other bank. You'll be high enough to see the car in its convoy and yet close enough to make the bullet count. It only needs to go into the engine block. Whatever damage it does will be enough to create the confusion we want."

"Where am I shooting from?" asked Galina,=.

"It's a college; they are always people going in and out. You'll be in a lecturer's office with a river facing window. The shot will be less than 1000 metres."

He pulled out a map from his pocket, "You can look this up properly on Google, but it's around here," he pointed to an area on the map.

"Why it's so close to your apartment you could almost walk to it," he said, "but oh, you'll have that heavy piece of luggage."

"What's the point of shooting at the car?" asked Galina. "Is something else going to happen?"

"No," said Theo, "It's enough, we just need to show that the people in the car are under threat of attack."

"No one gets hurt?" asked Galina.

"No, no one gets hurt," answered Theo, "This is a precision shot to create an incident. That's all."

Galina looked at me. "I'll need support," she bargained, "I'd like Alya to help me," she looked at Theo.

"The fees were set for this assignment, but I'll see what I can do, I know this means a lot to the client,"

"Good," said Galina, "Let me know the outcome. Then I'll confirm that I'm in."

He smiled, "A pleasure, as always," he said as he stood to leave.

He tucked a 50 Euro note under his cup. Enough for all of our coffees.

Galina looked back to me. "Sorry about that," she said, "But I wanted to see him squirm a bit, I should have asked you first."

I'm in," I said, "Let's see if I can get paid as well,"

We walked back to the apartment. Theo was right, it would take less than 20 minutes to walk to the building where the rifle was to be used.

e took the weapon's carry box out onto the balcony of the apartment. It seemed heavy even without the rifle in it. We laid the area with newspaper and pieces of cardboard and sprayed the very manly-looking gun-box into a pretty pink colour, with a couple of purple patterns on each side. Then I applied a few cut out stickers which we'd bought in the Brico' to the sides. Little flying unicorns and clouds on a pink background. Very pretty.

"Okay, we'll let that dry, then we have a perfect 'hidden in plain sight' situation."

We'd decided to leave Paris the next day, to go north around 100km on the A1 to Forêt de Compiègne. It was also the nearest large woodland that we could find, where we could test the rifle without being disturbed. The other nearby forests of Haute Vallée de Chevreuse Regional Natural Park and Gâtinais Français Natural Regional Park were crisscrossed with so many roads and were so close into Paris that locals and tourists alike would venture to them.

We'd also worked out that if the test was successful, we could make a day of it, continue on to Reims, pick up some champagne and then head back on the A4 into Paris.

We both said we felt like we were in a Frederick Forsyth novel and were waiting for a heavily disguised Bruce Willis to turn up. We decided against taking a watermelon.

The next day, we started early for Forêt de Compiègne. We soon found an area away from people and parked Galina's unassuming little Renault. We carried the big pink box to a field ditch. Then we had to build the weapon. I left it to Galina, who had it assembled in less than ten minutes. It looked suitably lethal once assembled.

Then we rigged up the rifle on its supports. Now to find a target. I'd brought some binoculars and spotted a tree in the distance. There was an overhanging branch which looked as if it would break when hit by a high-velocity shell.

I told Galina, and she took sight. There was a gentle breeze and so she adjusted the sights for drift. One squeeze of the trigger, a pause whilst the bullet travelled and then blam, we could see the branch judder from the impact. I looked through my spotter binoculars and could see that Galina had missed the branch but hit an adjacent area of tree. It had made a huge hole, where the shell's force had wiped through the tree's body.

"Wow," I said to Galina," That was so close, I think you've only got about 30cm of drift over 1000 metres."

"Okay, she said, "The second bullet is in the chamber. One more go," She appeared to concentrate and ever so gently squeezed the trigger. We waited for the bullet to reach the target.

Bam. This time the tree branch didn't just sway, it more or less exploded. We could see bark and leaves pattering to the ground. The branch had been cleanly cut in two.

"This is some rifle," said Galina, "It is a step up from the OM5-s"

"That was some serious shooting, Galina!" I replied. She'd done an amazing job with her second shot. I was less worried now about her ability to pull off the mission.

We were very aware of any passing people in the forest and decided we'd better pack up quickly now, before anyone spotted us or wondered about the distant tree.

Inside the car, Galina looked happy, but I could see she was still concerned.

"What is it?" I asked.

"Theo," she answered, "Can we really trust him? I don't mean about the money; I mean about whether anything is going to happen to the occupants of the car or the convoy when we attack it?"

"We've got little choice," I said, "But he knows that if he double crosses us or misleads us then he'll find himself at the wrong end our anger."

"Yes," nodded Galina, "Let's go find that champagne."

Next we had to decide on the get-in and get-out. We'd thought we'd be able to take the box to the room early and leave it under a pile of discarded cloth. Before we did so, we were going to load up the weapon with DNA. We did this by old-school tradecraft. We got one of those sticky rollers for getting hair off clothes and then ran it along a couple of metro carriages. Blech. We got more DNA than we would ever need. Galina got some surgical gloves. After we'd put the roller over the weapon, neither of us wanted to touch it again.

Then Theo called. A change of plan. We were not going

to use the college and the room. He said he had found somewhere better. A hotel - we could take the rifle in as part of the luggage. We were both worried at these last-minute changes. He said it would help him with logistics.

It came to the day. Theo made contact. He told us about the timings and the car to expect. It was to be at eleven o'clock in the morning. It was part of a convoy which was to move east along La Rive Droite. From television, we worked out it was part of a G8 working party convoy. We thought it would be filled with special advisors rather than the top people. The revised room that Theo had told us was a hotel room on the Quai Voltaire. Easier, although the hotel would have security cameras.

Galina's LBGT Friends helped us here. In a nearby Theatre's tiny changing room, we were soon transformed into a couple of cross-dressed slutty men, which could have formed a comedy duo. Either that or *Une nouvelle amie* - at least the French had an understanding for such behaviour.

It was a sensible precaution. Instead of adopting disguises, the hotel staff would remember us as two cross dressers. The descriptions given would be laughable.

We checked in, carried our bags and the rifle to our top floor room, and Galina set it up. It was barely 500 metres to our target, across the Seine. The cars would move along Quai Francoise Mitterand, accompanied helpfully by some leading motorcycles.

I helped Galina set up a table and pull the rifle back so that nothing showed from the outside. The silencer on the end of the rifle made the whole setup look even more menacing.

"Shall I order room service?" I said to Galina.

"Ta Gueule!" she answered; I could tell she was not amused.

Eleven o'clock approached.

We could see the car making its way along the riverbank. There was a whole procession of blue lights. I spotted for Galina, with a pair of binoculars. I could see the car. It had a little flag on the front.

"Got it," said Galina, as she prepared the weapon. I could hear her breathing. Then Blam, a noise so loud it startled us both. She'd fired on the car. The bullet took a moment to cross the river and then a metallic shudder. The whole car was knocked sideways by the round. Neither of us had expected that. We'd thought it would make a clean hole in the front of the car.

The commotion of squealing brakes, sirens and even some further handgun fire made its way across the river. We knew we needed to get out and slipped into the elevator. Downstairs the hotel staff were looking out of the front of the hotel.

"What is it?" I asked.

"Don't know, a car crash or something. It looks bad."

"We'd better go the other way," I said.

We walked right from the hotel, along the left bank and away from the commotion. We turned right on Rue Bonaparte and were soon back at our own apartment. We'd shed a few clothing items on the way, into our backpacks. By the time we arrived back at the apartment, we looked almost normal, certainly not oddly dressed in a way that would attract attention.

Galina tuned in the television to 24-hour news. There was a coverage of the event. There had been an explosion in the leading car of the convoy. It had lost control and crashed into the sidewalk. No-one was injured, but there was to be an investigation because it had security ramifications for the upcoming Summit.

From our apartment, we could hear the helicopters gathering around the scene.

We guessed this was the desired outcome. They would move the Summit to another city now. The news was not mentioning the rifle shot. We reckoned that would come out the next day, when they discovered the weapon.

Theo rang, "Hey girls," he said, patronisingly, "Good work, that was a short Summit," he said.

"What was it about?" asked Galina.

"Arms control," said Theo, "They'll need some extra pages after that, I think."

"What about when they find the rifle?" asked Galina.

"What rifle?" asked Theo, "I sent in a delivery man to collect the package, just after you left the building. He said it was very pink."

"So, you've moved the weapon?"

"Yes, it's gone, as have your two small luggage bags. You were never there, aside from what they have on the cameras - and I think that might disappear tonight," he said.

We looked at one another Theo had used a big team for this operation. It must have been well-sponsored although he would never tell us.

"Okay - I'll see you at the cafe, with the cash," he said, "Ciao Ciao."

Instead of a sense of relief, we were both concerned about the twists and turns of this last piece of work from Theo and the way that he was information hiding much of it from us.

We talked long into the night but eventually decided that this would need to be the end. We'd both had some fun, but now Theo knew where we lived, we were concerned that he could turn us in as part of operations. We couldn't work out who he operated for, an whether there was any sense of duty or conviction driving him.

We'd, literally, turned into hired guns. "Gun girls," as we suspected Theo would describe us.

Next day we met Theo at the cafe. It was early, but he was drinking Pastis, so we followed him and ordered two Absinth. We could all drink aniseed flavors although ours were just that hint more rebellious.

"Hi Ladies," he said," Here' are the envelopes. I divided it for you both." He handed the envelopes across underneath a copy of Le Figaro. We noticed the front page featured the incident from yesterday.

"I'm going away for a while," he said, "It's become difficult for me around here. Don't expect to hear from e efor a while."

With that, he stood, btipped back the last of his Pastis, owed towards us slightly formally and left,

It spooked us, and we looked around the cafe, in case there were any signs of movement or surveillance. We knew that Theo was good at his job, so we doubted he would have been followed.

It cemented our decision from the prior evening. We would split up. We both looked at one another.

"It's been good," said Galina - she was speaking Russian. *"ochen' khorosho - luchsheye - moya lyubov'* ", I replied.

We knew the best split was immediate and without explanations about our plans. We'd swapped a cover email address for the future but knew this was most likely it.

The next morning, I woke up. Galina had already gone.

I hurried to the Gare du Nord. Eurostar to London. Same name, but different country.

Hot

You will not grasp her with your mind
Or cover with a common label,
For Russia is one of a kind –
Believe in her, if you are able…

Fyodor Tyutchev - 1866

Coin

London. I was living in East London. It was slightly cheaper than out west, and hilariously hipster, but with a more European twist than the west side, which was stuffed with Russian money and gold-plated apartment blocks.

I decided to lie low and not do any work for a long time. I had my income from the FSB and I'd also amassed plenty of extra cash from the various assignments.

I was living just off Brick Lane, so had Shoreditch, Spitalfields and the towering chimney of an ex brewery turned gallery on my doorstep. There was a steady wash of tourists and Londoners through the area and I often heard Russian, and even Bulgarian and Icelandic being spoken.

To my great surprise, I even discovered that there was a farm about five minutes from where I lived. It wasn't anything like the size of the one we'd had back in Iceland, but it still kept sheep, goats and donkeys, so I could get my occasional fix of city farm tranquillity.

I needed it after the scary news report about Theo. He'd been found in the Seine. The report didn't go into much detail, but made it look as if he'd jumped from one of the bridges.

I didn't buy the story and I was sure that Galina wouldn't either. I decided not to contact her though. The secret email was for a real emergency use, not just because we'd heard something from our last assignment.

I speculated that Theo had been too elaborate with his plans for that rifle job. He'd had to get too many people involved. The cancelled college room, the hotel, obtaining the weapon, the weapon drop-off, the pickup, the room cleaning. He was leaving quite a trail. Even meeting us in Café de Flore twice, which we'd both thought wasn't tradecraft.

If I had to bet, it would be the college room that was the weak point. Fixing it with someone low-level, hiring a room and then them getting greedy. Theo cancels and the college room owner trades the information to make some money. I'll mark that as unfinished business. Theo might have been creepy, had a bit of an alcohol thing, but didn't deserve to be betrayed.

I'd been in London for around three months. I was in the process of restarting my music thing and had been practicing singing and guitar with a few people I'd met. I decided it was better to be purposeful rather than scenic.

That's when I was contacted about an assignment. This was from the FSB, but I was quite suspicious. I decided that the longer one was out of the game, the more unappealing the offers. This time it was babysitting a couple of operatives in London.

The Moscow handler was as obscure about the mission as Theo had been. I was to go to two different locations in London and to extract van drivers, who were to be taken away to another location by taxi. The taxi was also one of ours and I'd be in it until I collected the van driver. I was told I would need to run some light protection for the van driver and that the area that I'd be operating in would be under a major disturbance. The assignment was to do the same kind of manoeuvre twice, within a few days of one another.

I knew it would be hard to turn this job down. After all, the FSB were paying me a good retainer which was allowing me to live in London. In addition, they would pay me a good contract rate for each job. They knew I was good and even referred to me as Captain Voronin, which was itself a flattering flashback.

I agreed, and soon found myself in the middle of a bomb plot. I don't know why, but a couple of non-lethal bombs had been let off around London. I think they were at UK Security Services buildings. I had to extract the van driver who had delivered the bombs to the locations.

That's when the plan seemed shaky. I talked to the first driver - in Russian - but he couldn't understand me. I realised he was someone local that had been hired and I had to go on talking to him in English. The taxi driver was another problem. He didn't know London. Anyone who has lived there knows that is impossible for a black cab driver. They spend years doing 'The Knowledge' so they really know the streets. This one couldn't even get us back to around Hyde Park Corner without referring to his phone's sat nav.

The same thing happened with the second van driver and I realised that if this was FSB, then they were running the rest of the mission on a low budget. What was worse, was that they let my name slip into currency and the next thing I hear is that they have pulled in someone with my name, from the Russian Embassy. I still don't know whether this was one of the duplicate Katarina Voronin's which Russia seemed keen to deploy.

I think the local handler was skimming the fees for the work. My contract had been agreed directly with FSB in Moscow- who didn't tell much but at least were honest with the payment. The local guy seemed to run his own books. No great maths brain to work out he was pocketing some of the assignment fee.

His mistakes risked getting me into deep trouble, because there were all kinds of additional allegations against Voronin, all across the time that I was living in Paris. One of them included the bombing of a Dutch marketplace, which seemed indiscriminate, and not even something that the FSB would arrange.

It turned out to be linked with some kind of cyber currency laundering scheme, which the Russian government and bank were trying to chase down. I was simply caught up in the middle of it. It made me think twice about taking this kind of bluebird mission in the future.

And even as Alya Sokolov, I still hadn't met any of the other Katarina Voronins.

Amelia Brophy

I flipped my identity again after that situation. I asked FSB to provide me with two further identities as a consequence of the mess from that last operation.

They agreed, and I was given an Irish identity as Amelia Brophy and another English one as Christina Nott.

I decided to put Christina's identity away and to only use Amelia for the next couple of years. If I was kept out of the limelight during this time, then things should stabilise.

I hadn't allowed for the changes in Russia. The oligarchs were taking increasing control of the administration and Putin's friends were getting into high places in most of the administration. Putin was privately saying that he'd fix it so he could stay in power for many years.

So it didn't surprise me too much when an organised crime lord made contact with me. He was Russian and had cousins in the FSB and a son who was working his way through the Kremlin's Academy in Moscow.

I was cornered and had to do what they wanted. It was some kind of industrial scale money laundering and they wanted me to help manage the loose ends. It turned out that an American Colonel Manners and bunch of London-based Brits were digging around inside the processes.

I was tasked with some runner operations within this situation which I could only see leading to a big show-down between the Russians and some Arab based interests. The Russians owned the pipelines, and the Arabs provided much of the oil. What could possibly go wrong? Well, plenty it turned out, what with careless botched assassins waving guns in London and even a restaurant bomb, which blew a big hole in a street in Knightsbridge.

I had to figure out a way to escape from this mayhem. It was clear to me that the disciplines instilled back in Archangel were not being followed by these Russian gangsters. If anyone could wave a golden gun, then it would be these bling-laden people.

So I made my escape from the gangsters, and just kept driving north. Ironically, when I reached Manchester, I decided I could do worse than to take a flight back to Kevlavik. Yes, I would lie low in Iceland for a while. I couldn't use the Amelia Brophy passport there though, for fear of being traced. I'd have to go into Iceland as Christina Nott.

PART THREE

It's all about the music

I come completely from the mountains

(Ég kem alveg af fjöllum)

Icelandic saying

Christina Nott

It was many years since I'd been in Reykjavik, and yet the vibe around Laugavegur was still the same. Amusingly, there were also still Hnakki driving noisy cars around nowadays playing Aviccii and SHM instead of Basshunter.

And there was something really comfortable about being able to talk in Icelandic, although I noticed some language drift as new phrases had replaced the old. Fortunately, my hipster London speak could override most of it and everyone wanted to get some modern English idioms into their chat.

This is really the time when I decided to do what Galina had done so well in the Paris and the USA. She'd create a proper second realistic career. No, I didn't want to become an ice skater, but I thought I could reignite my music.

I knew I was too old for the full-on pop scene, but it shouldn't deter me from a more niche position. I used to know one of the members of a well-known band who was now on the local Reykjavik Council. I went along to a council meeting to meet him and he remembered me from the farm and my piano playing. I think as children we had formed a mini quartet with two others. He played the trumpet and sang, although in those days it was mostly Icelandic folk tunes.

I told him about my plans, and he looked me up and down.

"Well, you've got the packaging," he said, matter of factly. I blushed at this unexpected compliment.

Then we both laughed. "Don't worry," he said, "I got married a couple of years ago."

"Then we'd both better worry," I said regaining my composure.

"Look, I can put you in touch with some people in the business, but it's cut-throat."

"No," I said, "It can't be as cut-throat as where I've just come from."

"Can you sing? - Maybe play an instrument still?" he asked.

"Yes to both, I can sing, play guitar and piano, oh and Balalaika, " I answered.

"Huh?" he said to the last one.

"Yes, you'd be surprised how fast it can become."

That got me started on the path towards what became my singer/songwriter phase. I could write songs about things that had happened without giving too much away.

EST (Electro-shock-therapy), was about a relationship. *"You've always been high-voltage;You know how to rock the room"*

Then there was French Kiss-off, which was about the break-up with Galina, *"No letter on the table; No lipstick mirrored why. No bitter final reasoning; Couldn't tell what made her fly.".*

And the one overt one about the line of business, *"Not saying it's the Barbie full of pins, not sayin' it's your screams. Not sayin' that revolver shouldn't be; But some of ya, Some of ya, Some of ya stuff - ain't normal"*
There was even a song about being a Hitman.

To be honest, I was told to dial it back a bit after these early songs. They wanted me to be more disco and less punk. I realised that we can't all be Björk Guðmundsdóttir from Iceland and I had to make plans to return to London if I was to make a go of the music angle.

This became something of a lost time for me though. I did get to London, become involved in the music scene, with follow up invitations to recording studios in Manhattan and then Amsterdam.

One of my security assignments had led me into contact with a group of Brits who seemed to be running a media enterprise. I decided to make contact with them, under my Christina name, to see if they could help get me further along.

Sure enough, they had no recollection of my involvement

in a previous assignment, but they did have music contacts via someone called Clare, media contacts via Jake and a strong technical capability though Bigsy.

Clare took me out to a London pub one day and tried to warn me about the business. She said that their company - called The Triangle - could try to get me some gigs or a recording contract, but that I should be very careful that I didn't get conned or ripped off by someone along the way.

She gave me a copy of Elmore Leonard's book "Be Cool" and said that it was a fair representation of the business.

Clare seemed to be pretty straight-talking and we became good friends. They did get me some gigs, but I came to realise there was an awful lot more to their enterprise than at face value. I could not tell them about my special skills, although I did feel, from time to time, that they could really have used them.

I soon realised that 'Be Cool' was right though. Elmore Leonard's L.A. music scene was incredibly tough. Most people lied and were trying to get money from your purse. The Russian hitman in Elmore Leonard's portrayal was a little suspect though. I don't think he would have talked so much.

But Elmore got it right about the music business racket. Through Clare, I did get a couple of club tunes out as an EP, which was played around the dance scene, but then I was offered a recording contract in Amsterdam.

Clare's advice was, "It's good money but there's probably a scam in it somewhere. And don't agree to take any packages anywhere."

I flew from London to Amsterdam, slightly wary, not least in case it was a trap by someone from the past. It wasn't. They wanted me to sing on an album. It turned out to be a Factory-Pop gig, where they wanted other artists to copy the real artists, so that the music could be played royalty-free. It's died out since streaming but used to be a big business in the Netherlands. That was the scam. Ripping-off real artists.

Of course, I didn't realise this until I was in Amsterdam, and so I spent a couple of weeks going into a studio behind Damrak, where I was hit upon by stoner-musicians while I copied vocals from well-known artists. The tunes were then going to be played as the backing to car-commercials or in lobbies and coffee-bars as background music.

I stuck with it though, because I learned a lot about the recording process and could see a few of the real professionals in action, who could get a vocal down on one or two takes.

I stayed in a small room close to Damrak for the duration of this, collected my money and went back to my London flat.

I told Clare and the others about this. I think they were upset for me, and at one point I think they were going to dip into their company's funds to pay me some more money. I stopped them from doing this, but I couldn't tell them where I was getting my extra income from.

Today

Well, that brings me almost up to the moment. I've had to leave London again now. I helped Clare and the others on one of their side-projects. It involved me performing at a gig where all kinds of mayhem was unfolding.

I think I was identified there by an American Colonel. Chuck Manners, I think, was his name. A real hard player who we'd watched from the FSB for years. He knew me as Amelia Brophy, but it won't take him long to follow the trail back to Katarina Voronin.

So now I've had to change identity and country yet again, to shake off the last identification. It means I'm indebted to the FSB again.

It suits them to be able to deploy me occasionally now. They've given me my new passport and papers. They still refer to me as Captain, but it's gone back to Captain Dobrayadoch. I hope they are burning the trail to the more recent name, although I still get referenced inside FSB as Archangel.

You won't be getting any more music from me, just a few written-down song lyrics and the album produced by the gang and called "Singularity'. Ironic titling, maybe?

I won't be saying my next name here. I've a whole planet to explore, although I think somehow, I'll be somewhere that means I can still receive my pay cheque from the FSB.

Signing out, Archangel. x x x